What Reviewers Say About MJ Williamz's Work

"MJ Williamz, in her first romantic thriller has done an impressive job of building up the tension and suspense. Williamz has a firm grasp of keeping the reader guessing and quickly turning the pages to get to the bottom of the mystery. *Shots Fired* clearly shows the author's ability to spin an engaging tale."—*Lambda Literary*

"*Forbidden Passions* is 192 pages of bodice ripping antebellum erotica not so gently wrapped in the moistest, muskiest pantalets of lesbian horn dog high jinks ever written. Within the first few pages we're greeted with fluttering crotches, burning loins, and the swell of young breasts. But, the erotica connoisseur need not worry, the slow start is intentional, and the pace and heat picks up considerably from there."—*The Rainbow Reader*

T0152344

LOVE ON LIBERTY

Visit us at www.boldstrokesbooks.com

By the Author

Shots Fired

Forbidden Passions

Initiation by Desire

Speakeasy

Escapades

Sheltered Love

Summer Passion

Heartscapes

Love on Liberty

LOVE ON LIBERTY

by

MJ Williamz

2016

LOVE ON LIBERTY

ISBN 13: 978-1-62639-639-5

THIS TRADE PAPERBACK ORIGINAL IS PUBLISHED BY
BOLD STROKES BOOKS, INC.
P.O. BOX 249
VALLEY FALLS, NY 12185

FIRST EDITION: OCTOBER 2016

CREDITS
EDITOR: CINDY CRESAP
PRODUCTION DESIGN: SUSAN RAMUNDO
COVER DESIGN BY SHERI (GRAPHICARTIST2020@HOTMAIL.COM)

Acknowledgments

First and foremost, I want to thank my wife Laydin who keeps me focused and moving forward. Also, a very special thank you to Mike Dennis for his input and help on the Vietnam Era. One book in particular that really helped with this book was *Who Spoke Up? American Protest Against The War In Vietnam 1963–1975* by Nancy Zaroulis and Gerald Sullivan.

As always, I'd like to thank Radclyffe for giving me a place where my story can have a home. And a thanks to Cindy for working so hard to help me become a better writer.

Dedication

For Laydin—For Always

CHAPTER ONE

Tommy held hands with the woman next to her as the crowd gathered around the platform. The man on the platform lit a piece of paper on fire and held it above his head. The small gathering cheered as another draft card went up in smoke. Tommy loved to watch every time. It never got old. She looked to her right to see she was holding hands with Sheila, a new member of their community.

"Let's go back to my place," Tommy whispered in her ear.

Sheila's eyes grew wide, then she smiled and nodded. Tommy guided her through the people until they reached her tent. Once inside, she sat and pulled Sheila close and stroked her long blond hair.

"Wasn't that exciting?" Sheila said. "Michael is so brave to burn his draft card."

"Yes, he is. But more people need to do that. The war is wrong. I just think women should have to burn theirs, too."

"What do you mean?" Sheila's eyes were wide again.

"I just think women should have to fight, too. It's only fair. We want equal rights; we should have equal responsibilities."

"Oh, Tommy. I could never go to war. Maybe strong women like you, but not girls like me."

"Well, I wouldn't go to this war even if we did have equal rights. We don't belong in Vietnam."

"No, we don't. You're so smart."

"I'm not smart, necessarily. I just think a lot."

"Well, I think you're wonderful."

"Careful, kiddo," Tommy said. "You don't want to get too close. It's all about fun and freedom here."

"Oh, I know. But I can't help it. I really like you. I've seen you with other women. That doesn't bother me. I'm just so happy you picked me this time."

"I've had my eye on you since you got here," Tommy said.

"Yeah? That's nice to know." Sheila burrowed in deeper against Tommy.

"I just didn't know if you liked women."

"I like everyone," Sheila said.

Tommy tilted Sheila's head up and looked into her eyes. She saw a mixture of longing and fear.

"But you've never been with a woman, have you?"

"No, but I want to, Tommy. I want to be with you. Please believe me."

Tommy wanted to believe her. She was there in her tent with her, wasn't she? But Tommy didn't want her thinking just because they'd made love they were a couple or anything like that. Tommy wasn't looking to settle down.

Besides, what if, once they got started, Sheila decided she didn't like women after all? Then Tommy would have to cool her jets. And that wasn't easy to do once she was raring to go.

Sheila placed a small hand on Tommy's cheek.

"What is it?"

"I just hope you know what you want."

"I do. I want you. No strings attached. One night with you."

Tommy took her hand and kissed the palm. She was so soft and warm. Tommy closed her hand over Sheila's. She closed the distance between their faces and lowered her mouth to taste Sheila's.

Sheila's lips were also soft and warm. They molded to fit Tommy's. Tommy kissed her again. And again. Her heart started to race. She ran her tongue along Sheila's lips and Sheila opened them to let her inside.

Tommy thought her heart would explode in her chest. She allowed her tongue to explore all around Sheila's mouth. She tasted good, like cheap wine and pot. Tommy was about to lay Sheila down when someone pounded on her tent.

"We're heading into town to celebrate," a disembodied voice said. "Are you coming?"

Tommy swallowed hard. She was torn. She could go to town then pick up where they left off, but she wanted Sheila and was intent on having her right then. Still, she gave Sheila the option.

"What about it? Want to go to town?"

"Not particularly. Unless it's important to you."

Tommy looked at her briefly before calling out.

"Not this time. Thanks."

"We could have gone," Sheila said.

"We could have. Or we could stay here and do this."

"Which is what I wanted."

"Me, too."

She eased Sheila down onto her cot and knelt next to her. She resumed kissing her, slowly and tenderly.

"Are you okay?" she asked.

Sheila nodded.

Night was falling fast, and Tommy was tempted to light a candle to allow her to see better, but opted against it. She didn't need their shadows in the tent giving everyone a show. Instead, she focused hard on Sheila and simply waited until her eyes adjusted.

"Good," she said. "Now, if anything I do makes you uncomfortable, I want you to tell me, okay?"

"I will. But don't worry. I want this, Tommy. I swear to God I do."

It was Tommy's turn to nod. She had to trust her. And she wasn't about to try to walk away now. She saw Sheila's small body laid out on her bed and couldn't wait to strip her and see her naked. Sheila looked like she could be loved a hundred ways to Sunday, and Tommy planned on doing just that.

She kissed her again and allowed her hand to play up and down Sheila's belly. She was greeted with Sheila's sharp intake of breath.

"You like that, huh?" Tommy said.

"Yeah."

"So do I." She slipped her hand under the flimsy cotton blouse and touched the bare skin. "I like this better."

"Oh, yes."

"Your skin is so soft."

"So is your touch."

"Yeah? Good."

Tommy moved her hand up and lightly traced the base of a small breast. She wanted to caress it, then suck on it and knew she would in time, but she needed to move slowly. She had to be sure Sheila was okay every step of the way.

"Oh, Tommy. Oh, yes. That feels wonderful."

Tommy watched carefully for signs she was enjoying it. Words were one thing, but watching her legs bend and straighten told her she had her squirming in pleasure. She dragged her fingers along her chest and drew a circle around the other breast.

Sheila grabbed her hand and placed it directly on her breast. Tommy felt the small nipple poking her palm and grinned. She kissed Sheila as she massaged the small mound and pinched her nipple.

"You have an amazing body," Tommy said.

"I'm glad you like it."

"I do. Very much. Now sit up and let's get this shirt off you."

Sheila sat up and pulled the shirt over her head. Tommy didn't know if it was the night air or excitement that had her skin covered in goose pimples. Either way, she was beautiful in the dimly lit tent.

Tommy bent over her and kissed her again. She kissed down her neck and back to her lips, savoring every inch she touched. She moved her hand to the other breast and played with it while she kissed her.

She nibbled down her neck to her chest. She saw the swollen nub of a nipple under her mouth and blew on it gently.

"That's cold," Sheila said.

"Just seeing if it could get any harder."

"And?"

"I don't think so. I think they're as hard as they're going to get."

"Is that a bad thing?"

"Not at all," Tommy said. "It means you're very excited and I like that."

"I am. You're making me feel things I've never felt before."

"Good."

Tommy took a nipple and sucked it deep in her mouth. Half of Sheila's small breast came with it. Tommy ran her tongue over the tip of it. Its hard, yet soft texture felt wonderful. She needed more so sucked harder.

Sheila ran her fingers through Tommy's hair, holding her head in place. Tommy continued to suckle as she slid her hand down to Sheila's skirt. She rubbed her hand up and down one thigh, feeling the heat radiating through her thin skirt. She felt Sheila tense.

"You okay?"

"Yeah. Fine," Sheila said.

"You sure? Because I can still stop if you want me to."

"No. Please don't. I don't want you to."

"Then just relax, baby. Why did you tense up?"

"I don't know," Sheila said. "I think I just wasn't expecting to feel your hand there."

"That's not the only place you're going to feel me."

"I know. I'm ready for you."

"Okay."

Tommy kissed her again and moved her hand back to her breasts, with the thought that she needed to go slower still. Even though every inch of her ached to touch her, to feel her soft, warm pussy. She broke the kiss and replaced her hand with her mouth. Her breasts tasted delicious and fit so perfectly in her mouth.

Tommy slowly moved her hand back down to touch Sheila's thigh. This time there was no tensing up. Tommy lightly massaged her thigh, soft yet supple, through her skirt.

"Can we take this off?" Tommy asked.

Sheila nodded and arched her hips for Tommy to slide it down over them. She helped her peel off her panties and lay naked for Tommy's enjoyment.

"You're beautiful," Tommy said.

Sheila simply stared up at her. Tommy stood and quickly stripped out of her jeans and flannel shirt. She lay naked next to Sheila on the bed and pulled her close for a kiss as she entwined her leg with hers. The feel of Sheila's skin against her drove her wild.

As they kissed, Tommy moved her hand down to touch an inner thigh. This time, instead of tensing up, Sheila lowered her leg, leaving herself more open for Tommy. Tommy stroked the thigh up to where her legs met, feeling the moist heat radiating from within Sheila.

She brought her hand up and tentatively touched Sheila's clit. Sheila gasped.

"Still okay?" Tommy asked, unsure if she could stop at that point.

"Still okay. Better than okay. I need you, Tommy."

Tommy continued to rub Sheila's clit until Sheila cried out.

"Oh my God," Sheila said. "How did you make me feel like that?"

"We're not through yet," Tommy said.

She slipped her hand lower and entered Sheila. Just two fingers at first, then three. In and out and around and about she moved them as Sheila twisted and turned to greet every thrust.

"Do you like that?" Tommy said.

Sheila only nodded. Tommy sucked her breast again and continued to fuck her until Sheila grew still and then collapsed.

Tommy pulled Sheila to her. She wasn't much into basking in the afterglow, but made an exception this time.

Sheila propped herself up on an elbow.

"So how do I please you?"

"Don't worry about it," Tommy said. "I'm fine."

"Didn't that turn you on? Or no?"

"Of course it did, but I'm okay. Don't worry."

"I'm not worried, per se. But I really want to take care of you, to make you feel some of what you made me feel."

Sheila dragged her hand slowly down Tommy's firm belly.

"Is it that hard? Do you think I won't be able to?"

"It's not that," Tommy said. "It's just that, well, never mind. Okay, I'll lay back and you can please me any way you'd like."

Sheila started by sucking on Tommy's hard nipples. The sensation was amazing. Tommy's nipples were hardwired to her clit, so everything was at immediate attention.

"Oh, yeah, Sheila. That feels good. That feels real good."

Sheila kept sucking as she slid her hand between Tommy's legs. Tommy braced herself for fumbling, but was pleasantly surprised when she felt Sheila's hand on her swollen clit.

"Oh yeah, right there. Oh God, yes. That feels good."

Sheila continued to rub, and Tommy felt all her muscles tense up. She was teetering on the edge of reality, wanting to go over, to float into oblivion, but she couldn't. She closed her eyes hard and concentrated. She fought the urge to place her own hand over Sheila's to help her out. This was important to Sheila, but damn, she needed to get off.

Finally, Sheila hit just the right spot at just the right angle and Tommy felt the tension release as the waves of relief coursed through her veins. She bit her lip to keep from crying out. She reached down and took Sheila's hand.

"That was wonderful. Thank you."

"Was it enough though?"

"Yeah. One orgasm is usually all I'm good for."

Sheila lay down next to Tommy again. They were snuggling when they heard music outside.

"The group must be back from drinking," Tommy said. "Let's get dressed and go join them."

Tommy handed Sheila her clothes, then quickly doffed her own. She took Sheila's hand and led her toward the sound of the drums and guitar. It was a chilly night so Tommy wrapped her arm around Sheila and held her tight.

"You okay?" Tommy said.

"Yeah, just a little confused."

"What about?"

"I thought it was a one-night thing."

"It was. It's still the same night, right?" Tommy smiled.

"Right." Sheila smiled back at her.

As they stood listening to the music, someone passed a joint their way. Tommy took a deep hit off it and handed it to Sheila. The guy to Sheila's left had his own joint, so Sheila took another hit and passed it back to Tommy. She inhaled deeply and handed it to the woman on her right.

The mellow fell over Tommy. The world was gone save for the drumming and Sheila's hand. Everything else drifted away. Tommy found herself swaying to the music. She pulled Sheila to her and they danced together to the rhythm. The music was hypnotic and that, combined with the feeling of Sheila in her arms, made her feel warm and content.

She took Sheila back to her tent and made love to her again. She slowly took Sheila's clothes off and then her own. Everything seemed to be moving in slow motion, and the sensations were magnified. She felt the softness of Sheila's skin and the heat almost burned her.

"Baby, you're on fire," Tommy said.

"So are you. Take me again, Tommy."

Tommy watched as Sheila ran her hands up and down her arms, mesmerized, it seemed, by her actions.

"Sheila?" Tommy said.

"Hm?"

"You okay?"

"Never better. I can feel every pore in your skin, every bulge in your muscle. It's amazing."

"I know." Tommy kissed her then, and the tingling when their lips met was like electricity. She pulled back briefly. "Did you feel that?"

"I feel everything, Tommy. I love it. It's mind-blowing."

"Feel me, baby. Feel me now."

Tommy lay down on the bed and pulled Sheila with her. She rolled over on top of her and kissed her again, this time easing her tongue into her mouth. Her tongue was soft as it played around her own.

Between her need and the weed, Tommy was dizzy and breathless. She kissed down Sheila's body, tasting every inch of her. She tasted of sunshine and wind. Finally, Tommy was between Sheila's legs. She looked up at her.

"Are you okay?"

Sheila nodded.

"Make love to me, Tommy."

Tommy dipped her head and tasted the heady flavor of Sheila. She was musky and sweet and delicious. Tommy moved her tongue over every inch of her, lost in the tastes and sensations. She still felt the drum beats, as if the drums were playing right under her bed. Each timbre matched her heart beat, which was heavy and strong due to her arousal.

She glanced up to see Sheila playing with her nipples. That was a good sign. She was clearly enjoying the attention. Tommy slipped her fingers inside and felt a sea of liquid coating them. Sheila's juices flowed thick and warm. In rhythm with the drums, Tommy moved her fingers in and out. Sheila arched her back and took every plunge, urging Tommy onward. Tommy was in a frenzy herself by the time Sheila finally let herself go and soared toward her climax.

"Do you want me to taste you?" Sheila asked when she could breathe.

"Do you want to?"

"I want to make love to you, woman to woman."

"I want that, too. But you don't need to use your mouth if you don't want to."

"I'm curious," Sheila said. "I wonder how you taste."

"Then do it. Do whatever feels right, baby."

Sheila climbed between Tommy's legs and seemed unsure of how to proceed. Tommy lay there, swollen and drenched, wanting to cry out, to beg for Sheila to do something.

"You okay?" She asked.

"Yes. Sorry, but you're so beautiful down here. I didn't expect to think that. Your clit is big and shiny. Your lips are swollen and wet." She moved her hand over each area to demonstrate. "I don't know where to start."

Tommy fought to keep her patience in check. She didn't care where Sheila started as long as she did.

"Start where you want to, baby. Just pick a place. I need you now. I'm desperate."

Tommy didn't expect the hesitant strokes of Sheila's tongue to arouse her so. But arouse her they did. She was moaning and groaning as Sheila licked one area then another. Her tongue wasn't as skilled as many Tommy had experienced, but that made it all the hotter somehow. She was tentative, nervous, yet determined. Tommy finally had had enough experimenting.

"My clit, baby. Focus on my clit."

Sheila did just that. She sucked and licked Tommy's rock hard clit until Tommy pressed Sheila's face into it. She was so close. Just a little more, oh God, just a little more. Sheila persisted and Tommy felt her body tense up then turn to jelly as the orgasm cascaded over her.

CHAPTER TWO

Tommy awoke alone in the cool early morning air. Something had disturbed her. She peeked out the door of her tent to see Sheila making her way back to her area of the compound. She rolled over onto her back, feeling good. Sheila had been a pleasant partner for the evening, and Tommy was quite certain they both understood it had only been for one night. Though if the opportunity presented itself down the road for them to hook up again, she certainly wouldn't say no. Just not too soon. That could give Sheila the wrong impression.

She sat on her cot and loosened the long braid that ran down the center of her back. She brushed out her hair and looked in the mirror. Twenty-two years young and looking good, Tommy reflected that she had her whole life ahead of her. She wanted to be famous. She wanted the world to have heard of her as an activist against the war. Of course in order to truly become famous, her true identity would have to come out. Thomasina Benton, daughter of the president of Benton and Associates, the country's foremost land development company. She wasn't ready for that. She enjoyed being just Tommy for the moment. And living on a commune and loving whoever she chose to love. She had almost no responsibilities. Life was good.

Speaking of responsibilities, since she was up, she might as well go help prepare breakfast. Or at least see if they needed help. She braided her hair again before she crossed the compound to the mess hall only to find they had all the help they needed.

"Thanks for coming by though," Freddy, a young man with long blond hair said. "What are you doing up so early? You've usually got a bunny in your bed keeping your warm at this hour."

Tommy laughed.

"No one in my bed right now. So I thought I'd swing by. You guys have everything under control so I'll be on my way. Peace."

She walked out into the morning air. It was cool and crisp, but the blue sky indicated a warm day would evolve. She had nothing to do and no time to do it in. She wondered what she should do with the day. Fishing sounded good. There was a creek that ran on the outer banks of the compound. She crossed back to her tent and grabbed her gear. She had just exited her tent when she heard her name whispered loudly. She turned to see Martina calling to her.

"Where are you going?" Martina asked when she caught up to Tommy.

"I'm going fishing."

"May I come?"

"Do you fish?"

"Of course. Who doesn't?"

Tommy eyed her suspiciously. Martina was a beautiful young woman with dark eyes and darker hair. No one knew her age, but she was a tiny thing, barely standing over five feet. She had manners about her that indicated to Tommy that she'd never fished a day in her life. But the company would be nice, so she agreed to let her come along.

"What do you mean, 'who doesn't'?"

"What's to know? You throw the line in the water and wait for a bite. No sweat. Anyone could do it."

"I don't know about all that, but I'm willing to take you with me. I'll help you learn to fish."

Tommy grabbed another pole and they cut across the expanse of tents that made up the compound. They eventually came to a gurgling creek. The tall trees overhead blocked the sun and kept the air cool. Tommy was glad for her flannel shirt. She looked over at Martina.

"You ready to fish?" she said.

"Sure." Martina smiled at her. Her olive skin glowed and her dimples showed. Tommy felt the familiar stirring that happened when in the presence of attractive women. She smiled back at Martina.

"Okay, then. Let's get it on."

Tommy dug in the cool, damp earth until she found some small worms. She baited Marina's line first, then her own. She told Martina how to toss the line into the creek and was greeted with a sidelong glance.

"I have fished before, you know," Martina said.

"I didn't know. The way you acted…"

"It's cool. But don't worry about me. I'm good. You go find your place to fish, and I'll be fine here."

Tommy wandered upstream a bit, not so far that she couldn't see Martina, and cast her line. She slowly reeled it in. Nothing. She repeated the motion. This went on for some time until the sun had reached its peak and even the trees couldn't prevent its heat from beating down on them.

Tommy made her way back to Martina.

"Any luck?" she asked.

"Not yet."

"You want to head back to camp now?"

"Hell no. I'm just getting warmed up."

Tommy scratched her head. Who was this Martina? She'd seen her around and just thought of her as a hopelessly lost soul looking for a place to belong. But after the morning they'd just spent together, she seemed anything but hopeless.

"So, okay then. We'll keep fishing. But I've got to lose this shirt."

Tommy stripped out of her flannel, wearing only an undershirt.

Martina blushed and looked away.

"Sorry," Tommy said. "But I'm really hot. If this isn't cool, we can just go back to camp."

"Oh, no. It's fine," Martina said. "It's very nice, as a matter of fact."

Tommy felt her crotch clench. Was Martina flirting?

"I think I'll take my shirt off, too," Martina said. "Oh, that feels much better."

Tommy stared at the trim body in army pants and a bra. She looked good. Tommy's palms itched to touch, but they were on a fishing trip, not a fucking trip.

"Good," Tommy said when she could finally find her voice. "I'm glad you're comfortable now."

They went back to fishing. Tommy was spending more time looking downstream at Martina than the water, but she couldn't help it.

Suddenly, Martina squealed and pulled hard on her rod.

"Have you got one?" Tommy called.

"Yes."

"I'm on my way."

Tommy carefully chose her steps to get back to Martina as quickly as possible.

"Do you want me to take over?" Tommy asked.

"I think I've got it."

Tommy took the opportunity to admire Martina's physique yet again. Her arm muscles and stomach muscles clenched and rippled in her struggle with the fish. It was a sight to behold. Tommy didn't think she'd ever forget the sheer beauty she was witnessing.

When Martina finally got the trout out of the water, Tommy was shaken from her reverie and quickly grabbed the net. Together they got the fish off Martina's line and into the ice chest.

Martina, still apparently high from her catch, threw her arms around Tommy's neck and hugged her tight. Tommy wrapped her arms around the small, lithe body of Martina and pulled her close, reveling in the warmth.

"Good job," Tommy said when she finally pulled away.

"That was fun," Martina said. "Find me another worm?"

Tommy laughed.

"Sure thing."

She baited Martina's hook again and started picking her way upstream. The rocks were slick and she had to be careful. But she was preoccupied with thoughts of Martina, and she made a misstep on a rock and slipped into the cold creek water.

"Oh my God, are you okay?" called Martina.

Tommy couldn't answer. She was embarrassed and freezing and mad at herself for making a rookie maneuver. She tried to get some footing to stand up when she heard splashing and saw Martina working her way toward her.

"Be careful," Tommy yelled her way. "The rocks are slippery."

"I'm okay," Martina called back. She was only a few feet away then and she hit the same slick spot Tommy had hit. Martina fell face first into the water, right on top of Tommy. Tommy tried to brace both of them to keep them from getting wetter.

"Are you okay?" she asked.

"Fine, I guess."

Martina got her legs straight, but her hands were still in the water, one on either side of Tommy. Tommy was cold, her ass starting to go numb, but all she could think about was kissing Martina. Her face just inches away, her dark eyes pleading with her. But no. Tommy needed to get them both out of the water.

"Can you stand up straight?" Tommy asked.

"I think so."

Tommy helped brace Martina's upper body and eased her to a standing position. Martina offered her hand to Tommy, who refused it.

"I'll just pull you down with me again," Tommy said. Instead she managed to get to her hands and knees and push herself up to a standing position. She slushed out of the creek and to dry land.

"So I guess we should pack up and get us home where we can get some dry clothes on, right?" Martina said.

"That's up to you. We can take off our wet outer clothes and let them dry if you want. We can make a fire and cook our trout here. That'll keep us warm."

"Let's do that," Martina said. "Let's have a true adventure."

Tommy stripped out of her jeans and laid them over a log. Martina took her pants off and did the same. Tommy was wet. There was no denying it. She was wet, and it had nothing to do with falling in the creek. She wondered if Martina realized she was playing with fire. She wondered if she cared.

Tommy started a fire, then cleaned the fish. She fried it and tried to focus on eating as she sat there, half-naked with Martina.

"That was delicious," Martina said. "Thank you."

"I don't know if I've had enough. I'd like to fish some more."

"Well, I don't really want to get out there in my underwear and I know our clothes aren't dry yet."

"True. So what should we do?" Tommy knew what she wanted to do, but wanted to make sure Martina was on the same page.

"I want to lay down and enjoy this beautiful day."

"That sounds wonderful." Tommy laid on the pine needles, wiggling until she made it soft and warm. She was surprised when Martina snuggled right up against her.

"This is cozy," Tommy said.

"It's nice." Martina moved closer yet. "Am I crowding you?"

"No, not if this is really what you want."

"What do you mean?"

"I mean, if you want to be this close, I'm fine. If it's accidental, then yes, you're crowding me."

"I don't understand." Martina started to move away.

Tommy grabbed her and pulled her back, harder than she'd intended, and Martina ended up on top of her. Tommy swallowed hard. The feel of Martina's soft breasts pressed into her made her brain short-circuit. She wrapped a leg around Martina's, pulling her closer.

Martina's eyes darkened. Tommy stared into them, questioning her. She knew her own desire must show in her eyes and she needed to know what Martina wanted.

"You may as well kiss me," Martina said.

Tommy laughed, as much from nerves as in response to Martina's statement.

"I may as well?"

"I thought it sounded better than begging you to."

"You never have to beg." She put her hand behind Martina's head and guided her down until their mouths met. Martina's mouth was soft and pliable. It molded perfectly to Tommy's. Tommy's heart pounded as she ran her tongue over Martina's lips. When Martina opened her mouth for her and their tongues met, Tommy rolled over on top of her. She drew her knee up to press it into Martina and felt the warmth emanating from within. Martina closed her legs around Tommy's leg, and she rubbed against her.

Tommy opened her mouth wide and plunged her tongue into Martina's mouth. She was frantic with need. She had to have her. She moved her hand down her back to cup her small, firm ass. Martina's body was so petite. Everything about her called to Tommy, challenged her to be gentle as she claimed every inch of her.

She peeled off Martina's damp panties and tossed them over by her pants. She brought her hand around front and ran her fingers between her legs. She found Martina wet and ready.

"Oh, Martina. You feel amazing."

"Do me, Tommy. I want you to fuck me."

"I will, baby. Don't you worry about that."

Martina spread her legs wider and Tommy dipped her fingers inside her. She stroked the soft area that she found there. She kissed her passionately as she moved her fingers in and out, and soon Martina let out a cry that echoed through the woods. But Tommy wasn't through. Martina had come too soon for her. She withdrew her fingers and licked them clean, then kissed Martina hard on the mouth, sharing her flavor with her.

"You're delicious," Tommy said.

"I am."

Tommy put her hand on Martina's clit. It was small but hard, and Tommy knew it was ripe for the taking. She rubbed it lightly.

"Oh, Tommy, yes," Martina said.

"You like that? That feels good?"

"Hell yes. Don't stop."

Tommy kissed her again and continued to move her fingers over her clit. Martina broke the kiss to scream again as she reached another climax.

Tommy was sopping wet by this time. She needed to feel Martina's small fingers playing over her. She rolled onto her back and squirmed out of her underwear.

"Please, Martina. I need you."

Martina lifted Tommy's undershirt, exposing her small breasts to the elements. The breeze added to her excitement and her nipples could cut glass. When she felt Martina's warm breath on one, she almost cried out. Martina's tongue swirled around the tip of it, sending electrical currents to Tommy's clit.

Martina let go of Tommy's nipple and it felt cold and wet. Martina kissed down her belly until she was kneeling across her body. She lowered her head and licked the length of her.

"Oh yeah. That's it," Tommy said.

Martina was working at a slow, steady pace, taking Tommy higher with everything she did. Tommy lay there enjoying it until she realized the position Martina was in. She was completely exposed to her.

Tommy eased up on her elbows and buried her face between Martina's legs.

"Oh, Tommy," Martina cried. "How am I supposed to concentrate?"

"Do your best."

Martina went back to working on Tommy while Tommy continued to enjoy her feast. Tommy was so close, she could feel her muscles tensing up and knew she would come soon. Still she tried to focus on Martina who finally came, sending Tommy soaring over the edge after her.

Martina curled up in Tommy's arms and they lay together trying to catch their breath.

"What a way to spend an afternoon," Martina finally said.

"No kidding. That was my kind of fishing trip."

"We'll have to go again sometime."

Tommy felt her gut tighten. She enjoyed the free love of the compound and didn't want to be tied down to anyone. Martina was no exception. But did Martina think there was more to it than just a fun fuck?

"Hello?" Martina said. "Was it that bad that a repeat wouldn't be fun?"

"Oh, no. Nothing like that. It was a lot of fun. But it was just fun, you know?"

"I know. I'm not asking for anything more. I'm practically Jack's girl anyway. I'm not asking you for a commitment or anything."

"Oh, good. Then, hell yeah, we could do this again."

"Do you think our clothes are dry yet?"

"I doubt it, but I don't necessarily want to go back to camp half naked."

"It's not like most of the women haven't seen you like that already," Martina said.

Tommy laughed.

"Touché."

"Have you ever been with a man?" Martina asked.

"Nope."

"Then how do you know you don't like them?"

"I like them just fine. I just don't want to fuck one."

"But how do you know?"

Tommy thought about it. How do you explain it to someone who sleeps with both men and women?

"I don't know. They just don't do anything for me."

"I guess that makes sense. How long have you known you were a lesbian?"

"Since high school. I used to make out with my best friend."

"When was that, Tommy?"

"Oh no you don't." Tommy laughed. "No one asks me how old I am."

"No? Why not?"

"Age doesn't matter, does it? It's just a way for society to try to control us. They make us think if we're a certain age, we should be doing certain things. In reality, age doesn't matter. We should all be free to do what we want, regardless of how old we are. Don't you think?"

"I do think that. I just wondered."

"I suppose we really should be getting back to camp," Tommy said.

"Or we could fish some more."

"Fish? Or fuck?"

"Either way works for me. But I really meant fishing."

Tommy stood and helped Martina to her feet. They brushed each other off and found their underwear. Their pants were still damp, but they put them on and hit the creek again.

Their timing couldn't have been better. They each caught three more fish, which they put in the cooler to take back to camp. They walked back together in peaceful silence. When they got to the dining hall, Tommy went inside to drop off the fish for dinner and Martina walked back to her camp.

Tommy whistled quietly to herself as she made her way back to her tent.

CHAPTER THREE

Lieutenant Dolly Samson just finished mopping up one yeoman's vomit when she was called to mop up someone else's. Sick bay was full, and the stench of vomit mixed with the screams and groans of men in pain combined to threaten her own stomach's fortitude.

As she walked by one young man, he reached out and grabbed her hand.

"Sing to me, Samson," he said.

"No time right now, Dalton."

"You come back when things calm down?"

"I'll see. There's lots to be done. We should be docking soon. We'll get you boys off this ship and into a regular hospital."

Dalton dropped her hand, and she set about her business. She cursed the war that hurt all these young men, boys really. Barely old enough to drive, they were sent into this cruel new world called Vietnam and told to give their lives for what? Well, to keep communism from spreading. That was a worthy cause, anyway. Still, she hated to see these boys destroyed.

After cleaning up the various spots of vomit, Dolly decided to mop the whole floor. It was clean and smelled of antiseptic, a smell she absolutely loved.

"They say it looks like a large group of people will be meeting us on shore," Tawny Mitchells said.

"Really?" Dolly's heart sank. The only thing worse than all these sick and injured kids, were the protesters that hurled vile and hateful comments at them as they were taken off the ship.

"Maybe they're family and friends," Tawny said.

"I doubt it."

"Yeah, me, too."

They took their places in preparation for docking.

"What are you doing with your liberty?" Tawny asked.

"I don't know. Probably just hang out in town. My family's not near here."

"Yeah, me too."

"Maybe we should get a room together somewhere," Dolly suggested.

"That would be nice."

"Okay, we'll do that. As soon as the ship is empty."

The ship docked, and Tawny and Dolly joined the other nurses in making sure the wounded and sick got off the ship in a careful, orderly manner. There were ambulances on the dock waiting for them. Dolly worked as a guide, directing patients to one ambulance or another, depending on the intensity of wound or illness.

As she worked, Dolly tried to ignore the loud, ugly yelling coming from a group of young people just off the dock. Some were chanting, but most were just yelling obscenities at the group returning from Vietnam.

Dolly didn't understand the vehemence with which they screamed. She couldn't fathom what made them hate these young men so. They were only doing what their country had asked them to do. Nothing more. Nothing less. There was no reason to yell at them like this.

The wounded and sick had all been loaded into ambulances and sent to various area hospitals. Dolly breathed a sigh of relief. It was over for now. She was looking at her feet, seeing blood splatters on her white nurse's shoes. She wondered which poor kid they'd come from. She was lost in her thoughts and didn't see the woman with the long braid walk up to her.

"How dare you?" the woman said.

"How dare I what?"

"How dare you perpetuate a war that is wrong? You serve on this ship; you betray all that is right."

The woman was right up in Dolly's face, and she momentarily feared for her safety. The hatred and anger in the woman's blue eyes shook her to her core. She finally found her voice.

"I help young men who are hurt and sick. They need someone to care for them. How can I turn my back on them?"

"They shouldn't be there in the first place."

"I agree." Dolly tried to sound calm. "They are much too young to be fighting in this war, but they are and I'm proud to help save their lives."

"It's not our war. Those boys have options. They don't have to fight."

"But they do fight. And I'm here to help put them back together when they get injured."

"You're as guilty as the rest of them," the woman said. "You should be ashamed of yourself."

Over the rants of the woman in front of her, Dolly could hear the crowd. Their chanting and screaming had been replaced with singing. They sang "Blowing in the Wind," a known political protest song. It made her skin crawl. People should be there greeting the wounded veterans with cheers. Not with heckling. Dolly was just about to respond to the angry woman when a superior officer called to her.

"Samson. Fall in. Now."

She turned away from her tormentor and joined the rest of the crew in formation. She stood there waiting to be dismissed and wondered what her leave would be like. She imagined having a few drinks, maybe meeting a nice girl. She smiled inside. She could enjoy herself for a few days.

Finally dismissed, she followed the rest of her group as they left the ship. The braided woman was nowhere to be seen. She must have retreated into the crowd which was now singing "Where Have All the Flowers Gone." The singing was better than the obscenities, to be sure, but their choice of songs left much to be desired.

Dolly and Tawny carried their duffel bags to a nearby motel and checked into a room. They showered and changed into their civilian clothes.

"What now?" Tawny asked.

"I could use a drink."

"That sounds good."

They made their way down the noisy streets filled with sailors on leave. They found a little bar that looked like a hole in the wall.

"These usually have the best martinis," Dolly said.

"Lead the way."

Dolly walked in and waited a moment for her eyes to adjust to the dimly lit room. There was a bar along the back wall with a mirror behind it. Round tables filled the small room. A few tables were occupied, and there was a small group sitting at the bar. She led Tawny to the bar and ordered a martini, dirty, with an extra olive.

She waited while Tawny ordered then led her to an empty table.

"This is delicious," she said.

"You sure know what you like," Tawny said.

"That I do. What are you having?"

"A margarita. It just sounded good."

"Right on. Well, cheers." She lifted her glass and clinked it against Tawny's. They sat sipping their drinks, and with each new one they ordered, the room around them got louder. On her fourth martini and feeling quite buzzed, Dolly turned her attention to the fun-loving group at the bar. There were six of them and they seemed to be having the time of their lives. They were laughing and relaxed. Dolly was jealous. Her life was so regimented. But she'd chosen it and didn't regret it. She was just a little jealous at the moment.

She kept her focus on the group and soon was drawn to the leader, a woman with a sensual voice and an easy laugh. She had a braid of thick brown hair draped down her back. When Dolly caught her face in the mirror, she was shocked to see it was the woman from the pier. She didn't seem so terrifying now. She looked like any other young woman out with friends. Against her better judgment, Dolly approached the bartender.

"The woman with the braid," she said. "What's she drinking?"

"Jack and Coke."

"Please send her one from me."

Dolly sat back down and resumed talking to Tawny. In just a few minutes, the woman with the braid was at their table. It was clear she didn't recognize Dolly at first. She was all smiles and charms.

"Thanks for the drink," she said. "To what do I owe this?"

"Let's call it a peace offering," Dolly said.

"A what?" Then the flicker of recognition passed in her eyes. Her body tensed and Dolly was terrified she'd made a horrible mistake. "Oh. It's you. I didn't recognize you outside of your baby killing outfit."

"I don't kill babies."

"Our troops do."

"Sorry. Forget I bought you the drink. You can leave now."

The woman turned, but hesitated. She turned back and extended her hand.

"Okay. Truce."

Dolly looked at her hand for a moment, wondering if it was a trap. But she finally took it and shook.

"I'm Tommy," the woman said.

"Dolly."

"What the hell kind of name is Dolly?"

"What the hell kind of name is Tommy?"

"It's an old family name."

"So's Dolly."

"Fair enough."

"This is my friend Tawny," Dolly said.

"Nice to meet you. I'd introduce you to my friends, but I don't think that would be such a good idea."

"No. Probably not."

"So, should I sit? Or will we end up killing each other?"

"I think you should sit."

Tommy sat, and Dolly was drawn to her deep blue eyes and easy smile. She was infinitely attracted to her and wondered if she stood a chance at even a night with her. She had no idea if Tommy was attracted to women. And then there was Tawny. She couldn't very well take Tommy back to their room. She cautioned herself that she was getting way ahead of the game. She needed to just relax and enjoy a drink with her for now.

"So what do you do, Tommy?" she asked.

"I'm an activist."

"What else?"

"That's about it. No time for anything else. I'm really dedicated to the cause."

"That can't pay the bills," Dolly said.

"Not a lot of bills to pay on the commune."

"Wow. You actually live on a commune? What's that like?"

"It's cool, you know? Living in a community with like-minded people is where it's at."

"I can't imagine. I need the finer comforts of home, I think."

"And you get that on a ship?"

"True. I meant when I'm not on the ship."

"How do you do it, Dolly?"

"Do what?"

"How do you see kids blown to bits all the time and not lose your mind?"

"If I was a nurse in a regular hospital, I'd see terrible things too. It's not that different. I just think of our sick bay as a burn ward and wound ward all wrapped into one."

Tommy shook her head.

"Damn, the things you must see."

"I'd really rather not talk about it. I'm on liberty and would like to forget my job for a few days."

"Fair enough. So, where's home for you?"

"Atlanta. And you?"

"I'm from the East Coast."

"That's a broad statement."

"New York City, if you must know," Tommy said.

Dolly raised her eyebrows.

"New York City? My, that's a far cry from a commune."

"And now we're changing the subject again," Tommy said. "I don't like to talk about my past."

"Fair enough. No past for you. No work for me. So, what shall we talk about?"

"What's liberty look like for you? What do you like to do?"

Dolly fought the urge to say exactly what she'd been hoping for, a few drinks and a nice woman.

"Have a few drinks. Maybe meet people. Check out the local sites. Typical touristy things."

"There's lots to do around here. Have you seen the zoo?"

"Liberty just started today. I haven't had time to do anything but have a few drinks."

"And you met me. So that's another goal checked off. But I was thinking maybe I could take you to the zoo tomorrow."

"Are you sure? I mean, I'd love it if you really mean it."

"I do mean it." Her voice softened. "You seem like a really neat woman, Dolly."

"Thanks. So do you."

Dolly could swear she felt the air thicken in the room. She looked at Tommy and thought she surely had seen a desire in her eyes. Was it the martinis? Or was Tommy interested? It was so hard to tell. And Dolly had to be careful. She could lose her job if anyone found out she was gay. Tawny knew because she was gay, too. But Dolly couldn't be too blasé about who found out.

They finished their last drinks and Tommy stood.

"That's enough for me. Are you going to stick around for more or shall I walk you back to your motel?"

"It's late and I'm exhausted," Tawny said.

"Fair enough. I'll walk you back to your place."

They got back to their room and Tawny unlocked the door.

"I guess this is good night," Dolly said.

Tommy leaned on the doorframe, looking at ease.

"It doesn't have to be."

Dolly's heart skipped a beat.

"What do you mean?"

"I mean, if you like, you and I can get our own room and continue the night."

"Do you mean that?"

"I wouldn't have offered if I didn't."

Dolly was speechless. She stared into Tommy's eyes and realized it was desire she'd been seeing all night. It wasn't her imagination. Tommy wanted her as much as she wanted Tommy.

She moved into Tommy's arms and felt them tighten around her.

"So is that a yes?" Tommy said.

"It's a yes," Dolly whispered.

Tommy went to the office and got them a room for the night. Dolly enjoyed watching the soft sway of her hips as she walked off. She found herself trembling, even though the night was not that cold. She looked at Tawny who smiled at her.

"Have fun," Tawny said, then closed the door.

Tommy was back and took her in her arms again.

"You're shaking," she said.

"I don't know why."

"Are you scared? Having second thoughts? We don't have to do this."

"No. None of those things. I want this, Tommy. I want this so bad it hurts."

"Well, let me take the ache away," Tommy said.

She pulled her head up and looked into Dolly's eyes. Dolly looked up and saw passion burning in Tommy's. Her stomach did a somersault. She wanted Tommy desperately. But what was she thinking? Tommy was almost as much of an enemy as the Vietnamese. She shook her head. No, she must not think like that. She needed to focus only on the throbbing between her legs, and that throbbing was growing by the moment.

"Please do," Dolly said.

Tommy eased Dolly onto the bed. She got on her knee and took off first one shoe, then the other. Next, she peeled off Dolly's socks. Dolly sat watching these simple gestures and her arousal grew.

"I can take off my own clothes," she offered.

"I'm sure you can. But I enjoy doing this, so please don't deprive me."

"Then, by all means, continue."

The air was cool on Dolly's feet, and she felt ill at ease, not sure what to do with herself, but she told herself to relax and enjoy the experience.

"Lie back," Tommy said.

Dolly lay down on her back, and Tommy unzipped her slacks. Dolly arched her hips to allow Tommy to take them off. She lay there in her panties and shirt and felt exposed. Not in a bad way, but in a way that she was wide open for Tommy to do as she liked. She couldn't wait for Tommy to have her way with her.

Tommy got Dolly's shirt and bra off before finally dragging her panties down her legs. Dolly felt free. She was unencumbered by clothes. It was her as nature had made her. She dragged her hands over the length of her body, enjoying the reaction it had to her touch.

"Hey," Tommy said. "Save some of that for me."

"I will. Hurry up and get out of those clothes."

Dolly watched in admiration as Tommy made short order of stripping out of her clothes. Her body was every bit as gorgeous as she'd fantasized. She was long and lean, and Dolly couldn't wait to touch her. As Tommy stood by the bed, Dolly reached out a hand and dragged it over Tommy's belly, watching it ripple at her touch.

"Scoot over so I can join you," Tommy said.

Dolly moved over to her left and propped herself up on an elbow to look at Tommy, who lay there looking sexy as hell with her blue eyes darkened with lust and a body just made to make love to.

Dolly felt like she was on fire when Tommy moved her hand over the length of her. She felt that she would surely explode if Tommy didn't touch her soon. Or even if Tommy did touch her. She needed it and she needed it bad.

"Touch me, Tommy," she said.

"I am."

"No, I mean, really touch me. You know."

Tommy slipped her hand between her legs.

"You mean here?"

Dolly's breath caught. She was so wet. She was dripping. She needed Tommy to take care of her.

"Yes. That's it. Now, make me come or I'll make myself."

"I'd love to see that. I love to watch women please themselves."

Unable to stand her arousal much longer, Dolly placed her hand between her legs and rubbed her swollen clit. Oh dear God, that felt good. She closed her eyes and relaxed into a rhythm when Tommy grabbed her wrist.

Dolly's eyes shot open.

"What gives? I thought you said…"

"I did say that I love to watch a woman please herself, but not you. Not now. Right now, I'm going to fuck you until you come for me."

Tommy slid her fingers as deep as they could go inside Dolly, who writhed and gyrated on the bed, leading Tommy's fingers to where they felt best inside her. Tommy plunged her fingers in and twisted her hand as she pulled them out. Dolly was beside herself. She was so close to coming, but she needed something more. Her head was foggy and her muscles tense, but she wasn't finding release until she rubbed her clit again. This time Tommy didn't stop her. They worked together until Dolly's world crashed into tiny pieces as it exploded in orgasms.

She finally opened her eyes and saw Tommy staring down at her. The look in Tommy's eyes made her gut clench. There was longing, to be sure, but also pride. Every emotion showed in Tommy's eyes and Dolly liked that. She leaned in and kissed her. Their first kiss. It was soft and tender at first, but soon filled with the passion they were feeling. As they kissed, Dolly ran her hand between Tommy's legs. She was coated in thick liquid and Dolly easily slid inside.

She moved her fingers in and out in rhythm with Tommy's bucking until she felt Tommy quiver inside. She ran her fingers over Tommy's swollen clit, and Tommy issued a guttural moan as she climaxed.

"Who'd have thought?" Tommy pulled Dolly to her and held her close.

"Hmm?"

"Who'd have thought the navy nurse and the activist would end up in bed together?"

"I know. I'd have thought it. As soon as I saw you at the bar, I knew I wanted you."

"Yeah? Well, I saw you and thought the same until I recognized you." Tommy laughed.

"I'm glad we were able to put aside our differences."

"Me, too."

"So…" Dolly said. "Isn't this about when you take off?"

"You've got a pretty good handle on me, don't you? Well, for one thing, I paid for the room for a night, so I may as well stay the night. Two, I don't want to walk back to the commune at this hour, and three, I'm taking you to the zoo tomorrow so I may as well stay."

Dolly hoped the degree of her happiness didn't show on her face. She was incredibly excited. She really liked Tommy and was thrilled that she would spend the night and that she still planned to take her to the zoo.

Tommy was an interesting woman, Dolly pondered as she drifted off to sleep.

Chapter Four

Tommy woke up late the next morning. She heard the shower going, so settled to wait for her turn. She saw doughnuts on the table and walked over to help herself. She took a chocolate covered chocolate one that was delicious. She hadn't realized how hungry she was. She'd essentially drunk her dinner the previous night.

She helped herself to another doughnut just as the door to the bathroom opened and Dolly walked out smelling clean and fresh. Tommy crossed the room and took her in her arms.

"Good morning," she said.

"Good morning."

Tommy kissed her hard on the mouth, and Dolly's arms went around her neck, pulling her close.

"How did you sleep?" Dolly asked.

"Like a baby. And you?"

"I had a great night's sleep."

"Good. Are you ready for the zoo?"

"I will be when you are."

"Great. Let me get in the shower. I'll be out in a few minutes."

"Sounds good." Dolly patted Tommy on the ass as she disappeared into the bathroom.

Tommy smiled as she got in. She took her time as a hot shower was a luxury for her. She lathered up and rinsed off and wished Dolly was in there with her. She was in the mood to have her again.

She didn't know what was up with that, but instead of wanting to get as far away as possible, she wanted to spend as much time with her as she could. She was confused and somewhat scared, but she made herself accept her feelings and see where they led.

She walked out of the bathroom naked and was sad to see Dolly already dressed.

"What's wrong?" Dolly asked.

"I wanted to have you again."

"Well, that can be arranged. I just went down to my room to get some clothes while you were in the shower. But I can easily take them off."

Tommy stared at her, the longing in her almost too much. But if they wanted to get to the zoo, she figured they should get going.

"No, that's okay. Let's check out the zoo. Did you want to see if Tawny wants to go?"

"That's very nice of you, but I think she's going in search of lesbians today."

"In search of lesbians, huh?" Tommy laughed. "What exactly does that entail?"

"She's heard rumors of lesbian bars. She's going to try to find one. Though she's terrified she'll be seen."

"Why? It's a free country. She can be in a bar."

"It would cost her her job."

"Seriously?"

"Seriously."

"That's bullshit."

"It's reality. Not everyone is doing the free love thing like you."

"Well, they should," Tommy said. "It would make for a much happier world."

"Maybe." Dolly laughed. "But it's not how it works for now."

"Okay, well then it's just the two of us. Let's go catch a cab to the zoo."

"Tommy, may I ask you a question?"

"Sure. What's up?"

"Where do you get your money? I mean for the motel, the cab, the zoo? You don't have a job."

"Ah, another off limits topic. Sorry. I can't say."

"You can't or you won't?"

"Either way."

"You intrigue me, Tommy."

"So be it."

Tommy reached for Dolly's hand as they walked toward Main Street to catch a cab. Dolly quickly pulled away.

"What did I just tell you?" she said.

"Oh, yeah. Sorry. I just want to hold your hand."

"Well, you can in our motel room, but not in public."

"I like you, Dolly."

"Thanks. I like you, too."

"It just seemed natural. I want to be touching you constantly. Is that so wrong?"

"No. I get it. I really do. But I don't want to lose my job."

Tommy bit back a smart retort about helping baby killers. She preferred not to think about what Dolly did for a living and focus instead on the beautiful woman with her.

Tommy caught them a cab and held the door open for Dolly, who slid in and didn't object to Tommy's hand lightly brushing against her back. Tommy sat as close to Dolly as she thought she'd allow. She wanted to put her arm around her and hold her tight. She didn't understand it, but the desire was there. She reasoned that she just wanted to have sex with her again, but deep down it seemed like there may be more to it.

The cab dropped them off at the zoo and Tommy was curious to see what exhibits Dolly liked. Tommy's favorites were the snakes and the penguins. She couldn't wait to see what Dolly preferred.

The zoo was fairly empty, which Tommy took advantage of by touching Dolly as much as she could. She either stood so close they touched, or brushed into her as she walked behind her to read something. And each touch sent a lightning bolt of desire coursing through her.

Dolly was like a little kid at Christmas. Each exhibit made her squeal with delight. She loved the big cats and declared the polar bears her early favorites. Tommy guided her to the snakes and was pleasantly surprised to see that Dolly wasn't at all squeamish among the large reptiles.

"They're so cool," Dolly said.

"I love the snakes," Tommy said.

"I wonder why. Do you feel a connection with them?"

"I don't know. Maybe. Maybe I envy their freedom, you know? They're the predators so they pretty much run their own worlds. That would be a wonderful freedom."

"That's an interesting way to look at things."

Tommy shrugged. She didn't know what it was about the snakes, but she loved them.

They stopped for lunch and each had a burger. Tommy seldom ate meat since it would be too expensive to feed everyone at the commune. They usually ate vegetarian meals. The burger was delicious, and Tommy took her time savoring it.

"Are you enjoying yourself?" she said.

"Oh, yes. I'm having a wonderful time."

"Excellent. We still have a lot to see."

"I'm up for it if you are."

"Oh, yeah. I love the zoo. I come here kind of frequently. Well, once in a while anyway. It's a nice, peaceful place to get away to."

"So even you have to take a break sometimes, huh?"

"Yeah," Tommy said. "Even though the commune is supposed to be peaceful, and generally is, occasionally we get wanderers who don't fit in. That brings tension, and eventually we have to ask them to leave. I'm usually involved in all of that. When that happens, I come here to get away. I also come here when the war weighs too heavy on my mind. It's a place I can relax and breathe."

"I'm glad you have a place you can come," Dolly said. "That's important."

"What do you do on the ship?"

"I read. I read everything I can get my hands on. The ship has a pretty extensive library, actually."

"Oh, good. So you have an escape as well. I'm glad to hear that."

They finished lunch and started the rest of their journey. Dolly was particularly taken by the birds of prey exhibit.

"You want to talk about freedom," Dolly said. "These birds live it. Soaring high in the skies searching for prey. Wouldn't that be amazing?"

"It'd be pretty cool. But they have other birds of prey to be afraid of. I don't know if I could live my life in constant fear."

Dolly got silent, and Tommy feared she had said something wrong.

"What's up?" she said.

"Nothing."

"No. You're being quiet. Tell me what you're thinking."

"Just that bit about living your life in constant fear. That's what we do on the ship, Tommy. We're likely to get blown up at any time."

Tommy heard her voice shake. Public display of affection be damned. She pulled Dolly into her arms.

"Shh. It's okay. You're safe with me."

"I'm sorry," Dolly said. "I know how you feel about the war. I shouldn't talk about it."

"Hearing you talk about it only enforces my resolve. I can't support what you do, Dolly, but I can be here to help make your liberty as enjoyable as I can."

"I know. And I appreciate that."

"Okay, well let's enjoy this beautiful day some more. Come on."

They went about their way and finally got to the penguins. Tommy said nothing about how much she enjoyed the exhibit until Dolly once again squealed in delight.

"Oh my God. They're so cute."

"Aren't they adorable?"

"They are. I could stay here and watch them all day."

"The zoo doesn't close for a while. Let's find a bench and do just that."

They sat close on the bench. Not close enough for Tommy, but closer than she thought Dolly would allow. She'd take it.

After a while, Dolly stood.

"I think I've seen enough."

"Are you sure? I'm in no hurry."

"Neither am I. I just don't want you to get bored."

"I won't, but we can get going if you want."

"Yes. I think I'm ready."

"So, what now?" Tommy asked. "Do you want me to take you back to your room and head back to the commune?"

She held her breath waiting for the answer.

"Is that what you want?" Dolly said.

"I asked you first. What do you want?"

"I'd like to spend more time with you."

"So that's what we'll do. What do you want to do next then?"

Dolly blushed.

"I'd like to go back to the motel for a while."

Tommy enjoyed the flush on Dolly's face. She couldn't resist the temptation to tease her.

"And what will we do there?" she asked.

The blush deepened, and Dolly didn't answer. Instead, she gently nudged Tommy in the direction of the zoo entrance. They caught a cab back to the motel, and this time Tommy went to the office and got a room for several nights, hoping to spend as much time with Dolly as she could.

When they got to the room, Dolly sat on the bed.

"Thanks again for getting us our own room," she said.

"No problem." Tommy sat next to her and held her hand. She lightly stroked it, thinking how much she wanted to get her naked and have sex with her again. But something seemed to be bothering Dolly. "What's wrong, baby?"

"Baby?"

"Too soon?"

"No. I like it."

"Good. So, what's going on inside that beautiful mind of yours?"

"Nothing. I'm just nervous, I guess."

"Nervous? What about?"

"I don't know," Dolly said.

"It's not like we haven't been here before."

"I know, but I feel like I just begged you to have sex with me."

"How do you figure?"

"I don't know."

"Baby, you said you wanted to come back to the motel. Sure, I assumed that meant we'd do it again, but I want that as much as you do. You didn't beg me for that. And you never have to."

"Okay."

"Okay?"

Dolly nodded. Tommy put her hand under her chin and lowered her mouth to claim her lips.

"Better?" Tommy asked.

"Much." She reached up, pulled Tommy to her, and kissed her passionately.

"That's what I'm talkin' about," Tommy said when the kiss ended. They kissed again as Tommy got Dolly onto her back. She held her face in place with her hand on Dolly's jaw. She loved the feel of her jaw working as her tongue tangoed with her own.

Tommy's temperature was rising. She was sure she would overheat, such was her desire for Dolly. She unbuttoned her shirt and unhooked her bra, freeing Dolly's full breasts.

"Baby, I love your breasts," Tommy said.

"I'm glad." Dolly laid her head back on the pillow while Tommy played with her breasts.

"I could knead and suck on them all day."

"Please do."

"Mm." Tommy buried her head between the two soft mounds of flesh. "They're so big."

"Should I be self-conscious about that?" Dolly said.

"Oh, no. They're beautiful. Absolutely perfect. What size are you, if I may ask?"

"I'm a thirty-eight double D."

"Perfect. That's the perfect size, I've decided."

Dolly laughed.

"They kind of go with the rest of me. I'm not the smallest woman in the world, you know."

"No, you're not. I love your figure though. It's totally bitchin'. And at least you have one."

"I love your body, too, Tommy. And it fits you. You wouldn't look right with curves."

"I wouldn't, huh?" It was Tommy's turn to laugh. "That's good to know, since I can't do much about the body I have."

She went back to sucking and licking Dolly's breasts until she needed more. She unbuttoned and unzipped Dolly's slacks. Dolly kicked her shoes off, and together they got her undressed. Tommy stared at the vision before her.

"You are so beautiful," she said. She kissed her again as she dragged her hand over the voluptuousness of her body. She played with her breasts again before moving her hand lower to find heaven between her legs. She spread her lips and delved inside.

"How does that feel?" she asked.

"Wonderful, but I need more. Give me more, Tommy."

Tommy slipped another finger in and then another until she was sure Dolly would be full.

"Oh, my God, yes," Dolly said. "That feels out of sight."

"Right on. You gonna come for me, baby?"

"I am." Dolly tightened her grip around Tommy's neck. "Oh, God, yes I am."

"Now?" Tommy said, frantically pumping her hand in and out.

"Yes," Dolly cried as she pulled Tommy to her. Tommy felt her close around her fingers and smiled to herself. Pleasing Dolly was as fun as it was easy. She could get used to this.

Tommy slowly slid out from inside her and pulled her close.

"You're a lot of fun to…" Tommy searched for the right term. It didn't feel like just fucking and it was more than just having sex. "Make love to."

"Thanks. And now it's my turn. Get out of those clothes."

Tommy stood and disrobed under Dolly's watchful gaze. She felt her flesh sear as Dolly's focus fell to every newly exposed inch. She was soon naked and beyond ready. She laid back on the bed.

"Do your thing," she said.

"Oh, I will. And I'll do your thing, too."

"My thing would be most appreciative."

Dolly climbed between Tommy's legs, and Tommy could feel her gaze yet again burning into her.

"Do you like what you see?" she said.

"I do. Very much. You're beautiful, Tommy. I'm going to taste you now."

"Please. Please do. I need you so bad."

Dolly dragged her tongue along Tommy's clit, and Tommy clenched the sheets under her. The feelings coursing through her body were almost too much to bear. She closed her eyes and just allowed herself to feel.

Dolly moved her tongue to Tommy's center and lapped at the silky walls she found. Her tongue was long and she was able to lick deep inside Tommy.

Tommy could not hold still. She was moving all around on the bed, urging Dolly to fuck her faster and harder. Dolly finally moved her mouth back to Tommy's swollen clit. She took it in her mouth and sucked on it as she ran her tongue all over it. Tommy felt the energy forming in her core. There was nothing else but the ball of energy and the feel of Dolly's tongue. Soon, the ball erupted, shooting the energy throughout her body as she succumbed to Dolly's ministrations and came harder than she ever had before.

But Dolly wasn't done. She slid her fingers inside and urged Tommy to the edge again. When Tommy was teetering, Dolly once again sucked on her clit, and Tommy screamed as she climaxed again.

"You sure know your way around a woman's body," Tommy said.

"I guess most lesbians do," Dolly said.

"I suppose that's right," Tommy said.

"Aren't most of your partners skilled?"

"To a degree. A lot of them are just experimenting, you know?"

"Really? I think that would bother me."

"Why's that?"

"I don't know. It's hard enough to be a lesbian. I don't like fakers, I guess."

"They're not fakers, really. They just don't know if they like women or not. Dig?"

"Still."

"It's all about free love, baby. Do what feels good and who feels good."

Dolly was silent.

"What's up? Talk to me. What are you thinking?"

"I don't know. I just don't go around sleeping with whoever."

"I'm glad. That makes me happy to hear that."

"Why? Clearly, I don't fit into your repertoire."

"Easy, baby. It's not like I have a set of rules you need to follow to be with me. I just think if it feels good, do it. And you feel good. The fact that I'm not one of many for you makes me feel special."

"You're different, Tommy. That's for sure."

"As are you. I could really get into you."

"Yeah?"

"Yeah. Now quit worrying about life and just relax."

They dozed together, enjoying an afternoon nap.

Chapter Five

Dolly woke, safe in Tommy's arms. She tried to disentangle herself without waking Tommy, but it wasn't going to happen. So she just lay there thinking. Mostly, she thought about the conversation they'd had just before they fell asleep. Why did it bother her so that Tommy was all about free love? After all, wasn't that what she was enjoying with her? Free love. No commitment. Soon, Dolly would get back on the ship, and Tommy would stay here and in no time they'd forget about each other. Right? Dolly knew that wasn't right. She'd never forget about Tommy. There was something about her that really drew Dolly to her. If Dolly didn't know better, she'd think she was falling in love. But that was ridiculous. She'd only known her a day. Still, that was Dolly's way of doing things. She fell hard fast and got hurt easily. She told herself to protect her heart from Tommy. If it wasn't too late.

Tommy stirred and Dolly held her breath, not wanting to disturb her. She rolled over toward Dolly and pulled her close.

"Hey, baby."

"Hey."

"You okay?" Tommy said.

"Yeah. I'm fine, why?"

"Just checkin'. Want to make sure everything's groovy."

"Everything is."

"Good. I like to hear that." She sat up and Dolly admired her physique from her waist up. She was muscular yet soft with small breasts that begged for more attention. Dolly felt like she could make love with Tommy for the rest of her liberty and not do anything else. "So, what's next on the agenda?"

Dolly kissed Tommy and moved her hand up to cup Tommy's breast.

"Whoa," Tommy said. "Someone's in a mood."

"You're just too fine for me to keep my hands off you."

"I'm not complaining. Not at all. If you want more, I'm always up for that."

They made love again and again, until they were about to fall asleep again.

"No," Tommy said. "No sleep yet."

"But I'm so relaxed," Dolly said.

"So am I, but I'm also famished. Get up. We need to take a shower and I'll take you out to dinner."

They took a shower together, which quickly turned into another lovemaking session when Tommy insisted on lathering up Dolly. When she ran her soapy fingers between her legs, Dolly had to lean against the wall for support.

Tommy was relentless with her rubbing, and soon Dolly was holding on to Tommy for dear life as her world was rocked by the strength of the orgasm.

Dolly dropped to her knees and buried her face between Tommy's legs. She was loving the feel of the water cascading over her body as she loved Tommy with her mouth. Tommy soon dug her fingers into Dolly's shoulders as she finally achieved the release she needed.

They stepped out of the shower and Dolly's legs were wobbly.

"I'm having a hard time standing," she said.

"I'm with you, baby. My legs are like rubber. You did me good."

They dried off and Tommy looked at her clothes.

"I really should get some different clothes to wear," she said.

Dolly's heart stopped. Would she leave her to go back to the commune? She didn't want to let her out of her sight. What if she left and didn't come back? She felt her chest tightening.

"What?" Tommy asked. "Don't you like shopping?"

"Shopping?" Dolly was confused.

"Sure. I just need to pick up a few things. Let's get dressed and we can go do that."

Dolly breathed a sigh of relief. Shopping with Tommy sounded fun.

"Okay. But, again, how will you pay for them?"

"And again, I'll write a check. You don't need to worry your pretty little head about a thing, baby."

"Okay. If you say so."

"I do. Now come on. Let's bug out."

They caught a taxi to Macy's and when they got out, Dolly automatically smoothed her clothes. She hoped she looked okay to go into the department store. Then she looked at Tommy in her jeans and flannel shirt. She seemed perfectly comfortable. Dolly was just being ridiculous again.

Dolly almost took Tommy's hand as they walked into the store. She just about fainted. What was she thinking? That would get her discharged. Still, it had seemed like such a natural thing to do. She wondered briefly if there would ever be a time where gay people would be free to be open with their lovers. She doubted it.

They were in and out in no time. Tommy didn't waste time. She marched into the men's department and grabbed some jeans, some slacks, and a few new shirts. She was ready to go while Dolly was still lost in her thoughts.

"That was amazing. You shop faster than any woman I know."

"That's because I think shopping is a total drag. So I get in, get it done, and get the hell out of there."

"Okay, so let's get back to the motel where you can change and then we can have dinner."

"Sounds good to me. Let's do it."

Tommy made short order of changing.

"How do those clothes fit you perfectly? You didn't even try them on," Dolly said.

"I know what size I wear."

"Yeah, but still, different styles can mean different sizes."

"Not for me. Now are you ready?"

Dolly looked down at her slacks and shirt and then at Tommy in hers. Tommy seemed so much more dressed up than she did.

"Let me change into a dress," Dolly said.

"Cool. Don't mind me. I'll just be sitting here watching."

Dolly felt the blush start on her chest and make its way up her face.

"You're so cute when you blush," Tommy said, only deepening the blush.

"I'm glad you think so. It embarrasses me."

"Which only makes you cuter. Don't ever change, Dolly."

Something about the way she said those words made Dolly pause.

"Do you mean that?" Dolly asked.

"I do. You're a special person, a real one of a kind. I like that about you."

"But there's so much about me you don't like."

"I don't like what you do. This is true. But you do it with as much conviction as I do what I do. That counts for something."

Dolly felt her eyes tear up. She fought to stop them from teeming over, but was unsuccessful. They rolled down her cheeks, unabated.

"What's wrong?" Tommy got up from her chair and took her in her arms.

"Nothing. That was just the sweetest thing you could have said to me." Dolly began to sob, the relief of knowing Tommy could appreciate what she did on some level overwhelming.

"Oh, baby." Tommy stroked her hair. "It's true. I meant every word of it."

"Thank you."

Dolly allowed herself to be held for several minutes, until her stomach growled and reminded her she was hungry.

Tommy stepped away.

"You should probably finish getting ready now," she said.

"I know."

Dolly went to the bathroom to splash cold water on her face then quickly changed into a skirt and blouse.

"Foxy lady," Tommy said.

"You're going to make me blush again."

"Great. I think it's cute how you blush."

"I don't."

"I don't think you see yourself as awesome as you are. I think you have too many insecurities. You need to let them go, man. Don't be so uptight. Just relax. Because, like I said, you're a wonderful woman. You need to believe that, dig?"

Dolly nodded, not trusting her voice. She was overcome with emotion. If she'd doubted her feelings for Tommy before, she no longer did. She loved her. And her heart felt like it would burst from all the love she had for her. She wished she could tell her, but didn't want to scare her off.

"Let's go. I'm starving," Tommy said.

She took them to a hole in the wall Italian restaurant and was greeted by the host by name.

"How often do you come here?" Dolly asked. She was perplexed at how a person living on a commune would be known at a restaurant in town.

"I get here once in a while."

"But the host knows your name. You've got to get here more often than once in a while."

"Not really. I suppose he remembers me because I'm a good tipper. I don't know. I do get here every so often though. You know, commune food gets old after a while."

"So you're a snob hippie?" Dolly laughed.

Tommy acted indignant, but soon smiled back at Dolly.

"I suppose I am."

"And you have the funds to pay for nice things," Dolly said. "So you could take others from your commune with you. Do you do that?"

"Sometimes. It depends on my mood. Sometimes I just need to be alone. Sometimes I want a date. Sometimes I just want to take some friends to dinner. So it depends."

"Are you ever going to tell me where your money comes from?" Dolly asked.

Tommy stared at the bread in front of her. She turned it this way and that, apparently weighing her answer.

"Not yet. Maybe soon. Probably soon. But not yet."

"Why not?"

"I'm not ready."

"Do you rob banks?" Dolly said.

"No, nothing like that. It's all legal."

"Then why not tell me?"

"I don't want you to judge me. And I can't have anyone on the commune finding out."

"I could never judge you, Tommy. If I was a judgmental person, I never would have bought you that drink as a peace offering."

"I suppose that's true," Tommy said. "Still, I don't want you to resent me or anything."

"How could I? I'm crazy about you. I won't resent you."

"You're crazy about me? Really?"

"Well, no kidding. Haven't you noticed?"

"I wasn't sure. Baby, that makes me so happy."

"Yeah?" Dolly said.

"Yeah. 'Cause I'm crazy about you, too."

"Really? I never hoped to dream you would be."

"Hell yeah. I don't spend this much time with anyone," Tommy said. "I'm pretty much a loner. I mean, I do things with others, don't get me wrong, but I always make sure I have alone time. So far, I haven't found that I need that with you."

"Well, that's a good thing. That makes me happy to hear."

"Good. I like making you happy," Tommy said. "I wish I could hold your hand right now."

"I know, but it's too dangerous."

"That's probably the best thing about living on a commune. No one judges you. You do what you want with whoever you want."

Dolly felt a pang of jealousy. She didn't like thinking about Tommy making love with other women.

"That does sound nice," she managed. "I mean not having to worry about being judged anyway."

"Is something wrong?"

"No."

"You sure? You look sad."

Dolly decided to bite the bullet and say what was on her mind.

"I just don't like thinking of you with other women," she said.

Tommy leaned back in her chair and laced her fingers behind her head. Dolly held her breath, terrified of what Tommy might say.

"I can see that," Tommy said. "I don't like the idea of you with other women either. But you don't have to worry. While you're on liberty, I'm yours and yours alone."

But what about after liberty, Dolly wondered. She decided not to press it. For now, she had Tommy. Besides, how could there possibly be a future for them? She was a navy nurse and Tommy despised anything military. She pushed the thoughts out of her head. She would simply enjoy the time they had and not worry about the future.

Dinner arrived and they spoke rarely as they enjoyed their meal. The wine had given Dolly a buzz, and she felt her face flush in the warm glow of the candlelight.

"You look beautiful," Tommy said in between bites.

"That was random."

"I can't help it. The candlelight is very flattering to you."

Dolly blushed.

"Thank you."

"You're welcome. How's your dinner?"

"Delicious."

"These little known places usually have the best food," Tommy said.

"That's so true. Thank you for introducing this to me. If I'm ever here again I'll definitely come back."

She grew silent. The reality that she would be leaving in a few days and most likely would never see Tommy again weighed heavy on her mind.

"Penny for your thoughts?" Tommy said.

"They're not worth a penny."

"Try me."

"I was just thinking how I'll probably never get back here to this restaurant again."

"Just the restaurant? That's all you're thinking about?"

"No."

"Baby, just relax. Let it be. We have now. We'll worry about the future later, okay?"

That sounded like Tommy was thinking of their future, too. Dolly relaxed a little.

The bill came and Tommy paid it. Dolly was growing more and more curious about where Tommy's money came from, but Tommy had made it clear that subject was off limits. Still, she couldn't resist another question.

"So, do your friends on the commune know you have this kind of money?" she asked.

"Nope. And they won't find out. Normally, I live quite modestly."

"I'd imagine on the commune, you'd have to."

"Yep. No need for frills or anything. Nice things would be wasted there. We're not into society's idea that you have to be better than everyone else."

"But you are," Dolly said. "Better than everyone else, I mean."

"Aw. Thanks, baby. So are you."

Tommy nudged Dolly with her shoulder as they left the restaurant. Dolly appreciated the physical contact. The need to constantly touch Tommy was almost painful. She wished she lived in a perfect world where no one would care. But that wasn't how it was. Homosexuality was wrong according to society and especially the military. She didn't want to risk a court-martial.

They walked a few blocks, enjoying the night air.

"We could walk back to the motel," Dolly said. "It might take a while, but we could do it."

"We could do that, but we'd have to go through some skuzzy parts of town. And I don't want you in danger. We're okay here, but we'll hail a cab soon."

"Fair enough."

They wandered along, looking at store window displays and simply enjoying being together when Tommy grabbed Dolly's arm. Dolly's first response was to pull away, but Tommy held tight.

"We've got trouble," Tommy whispered.

Dolly followed Tommy's line of sight and saw the group of young men approaching them.

"Be calm," Tommy said as she led Dolly backward. "Don't panic."

The men started running toward them and Tommy hailed a cab just in time. She forced Dolly in and climbed in after. The cab sped off, and Dolly collapsed against Tommy, fighting tears.

"That was scary," she said when she finally found her voice.

Tommy put her arm around her, holding her tight.

"I thought we still had a block or two of safety. I'm sorry. I never should have let us get into that situation."

"It's okay. We're safe now." Dolly realized the position she was in and forced herself to a sitting position well out of reach of Tommy's arms. She hoped the driver hadn't noticed them.

Tommy adjusted the way she was sitting as well.

"Yes, we are. I promise not to let that happen again."

The taxi dropped them off at the motel, and Tommy quickly unlocked the door, looking around as she did.

"There's no way they could have followed us," Dolly said.

"I know. I'm just being paranoid. But I feel awful for putting you in danger."

"It's over, Tommy. Relax."

"I'm afraid I'm too freaked out to relax. I need a drink."

"Do you want to go back out to a bar?"

"No. I saw a liquor store around the corner. I'll go get some booze. You want anything?"

"I'll have some more wine," Dolly said.

"Okay. I'll be right back."

Dolly waited for Tommy to come back. She turned on the old television in the room and tried to follow the story line of an old movie. She started to get worried. How long had Tommy been gone? She paced back and forth in the room. Tommy had been gone too long. Something was wrong. She needed to go see what had happened.

She was just putting her jacket on when she heard the key in the slot. The door opened and Tommy walked in. Dolly threw her arms around her and pulled her close.

"What took so long?" she said.

"I had to find just the right bottle of wine for you. I didn't just want to pick up some cheap shit."

"Well, you were gone forever. I was worried sick."

"I'm sorry, baby." She kissed Dolly. "Now, I'm gonna make a drink. Let me open that bottle of wine for you."

"We don't have a corkscrew."

"I bought one. Don't worry. I think I thought of everything."

"You're the best."

"Thanks, baby."

Tommy went over to her flannel shirt and reached into the pocket. She pulled out a joint.

"What are you doing?" Dolly said.

"Have you ever toked?" Tommy said.

"Never. I'd get kicked out of the navy."

"Who's gonna know?"

"I will."

"Yeah, but they won't. Come on. It'll help you relax."

Tommy lit the joint and took a deep drag off it. She handed it to Dolly who did the same, only to end up in an extreme coughing fit.

"Easy there," Tommy said. "You're not used to it. Little tokes for you, baby."

Dolly was still coughing as she handed the joint back to Tommy. Tommy took another hit and gave it back to Dolly.

"Remember, little hits."

Dolly took a small puff.

"There you go," Tommy said. "That should do it."

Dolly sat back with her glass of wine, feeling mellow and relaxed, the events of the night fading deep into the recesses of her memory.

CHAPTER SIX

Dolly tried to feel guilty for smoking the marijuana, but she didn't have the energy. She sat back in her chair and noticed the brightness of the television screen and observed every thread in the old curtains. Everything seemed magnified and beautiful. She felt light-headed, but it was okay. It didn't matter. Nothing mattered.

She watched as Tommy crossed the room to her. She cut through the air as if cutting through water. She seemed to be moving in slow motion.

"So this is what stoned is like?" Dolly said.

Tommy laughed at the question.

"Yep. Pretty cool, huh?"

"Weird. Dry mouth."

"Yeah. That happens. Sip some wine. You'll be fine."

"You feel better, too?" Dolly was having a hard time forming sentences, but she focused really hard to make them make sense.

"I do. I'm much more relaxed now."

"You talk so easy," Dolly said.

"Huh?"

"My thoughts won't come."

"Sure they will. You're thinking."

"But can't say that."

Tommy was laughing.

"Can't say what, baby?"

"My thoughts." She paused. "Can't make it to my mouth."

"Ah. Yeah. That can happen the first couple of times. But it's cool. Just relax. Let it be. You don't have to say anything. Just be."

Dolly thought how stupid she sounded and couldn't stifle a giggle. She tried, but it burst right out, followed by another. She looked up to see Tommy smiling down at her and she lost it. She started laughing hysterically, so hard she had to fight to catch her breath.

Tommy joined in and the two of them laughed for what seemed an eternity. Tommy finally stroked Dolly's hair.

"See? Being stoned is fun."

"Yeah, it is. I want more."

"Oh, no you don't. You've had just the right amount. You won't need any more for a while. Probably not tonight."

"But it feels so good."

"And it will. The feeling lasts a long time. Trust me. Can I get you another glass of wine?"

Dolly looked down and saw the empty glass in her hand. She hadn't realized she'd finished it.

"Please," she said.

Tommy crossed over to the dresser and poured them each a drink. She carried them back and gave Dolly her wine. She watched Dolly take a sip.

"This is good wine," Dolly said.

"Nothing but the best for my baby."

"You're so sweet."

Tommy kissed her then, and Dolly was intensely aware of the flavor of Jack Daniels mixed with her red wine. The combination should have been repulsive, she thought, but it worked. It was a bringing together of the two of them and that was a good thing.

Tommy's tongue was fluid as it moved around Dolly's mouth. Every inch it touched came alive. She tried to keep up with it, but found herself too stoned to be that coordinated. Instead she did her best to follow it around. Either way, Tommy had her more turned on than she'd ever been in her life. The long, slow kissing was drawing out her arousal, and she loved the way she felt.

Dolly gave Tommy her glass of wine and stood uneasily from the chair. Tommy set their drinks down and pulled Dolly into her arms.

"You feelin' okay?" Tommy asked.

"Never better."

"Right on."

Tommy pulled Dolly's blouse over her head and kissed her again. Her kisses were slow and languid, and Dolly's head felt lighter still. Tommy unhooked her bra and slid it down her arms.

"Why do you wear these?" Tommy asked.

"What?"

"Bras?"

"I kind of need to," Dolly said.

"No, you don't. They're contraptions that society says women must wear. You don't have to wear one."

Dolly wanted to argue, but couldn't find the words. She wanted to tell Tommy that the size of her breasts made it painful to have them free all the time. She wanted to tell her it was regulation in the navy that she wear one. She tried to formulate the sentence, but her mind was too fuzzy.

"Yes, I do," was all she could say.

"Why? Because you have such large breasts?"

"Yes. It would hurt."

"Would it really?" Tommy said.

"Yes."

"Okay then. That makes sense."

Tommy cupped Dolly's breasts. The feel of her warm skin against Dolly's cool flesh made her nipples tighten. She knew Tommy knew how to please her and that she would be begging for release soon. She just needed to relax and enjoy the slowness with which everything was happening.

Dolly fumbled with the button on her skirt and finally got it undone. The zipper was easy, but stepping out of the skirt proved challenging. She almost fell over several times. Finally, she put her hands on Tommy's shoulders to brace herself and she stepped out of it.

Tommy was laughing at her, but it was okay. It sounded like she was far away and it wasn't hurtful. Dolly thought about how she must have looked falling over like that, and she started laughing, too. Soon, she fell onto the bed, laughing hysterically.

When she caught her breath, she looked up to see Tommy looking down at her. She wasn't laughing anymore, but she had a smile on her face.

"What?" Dolly said.

"You're beautiful. And you're fun when you're stoned."

"I am?"

"Yes, you are. You're funny."

"I couldn't...my skirt...almost fell..."

"I know. I saw." Tommy started laughing again. "But you're fine now and you're lying on the bed and now I need to have you."

"Okay." Dolly tried to make herself stop giggling.

Tommy stripped out of her clothes and peeled Dolly's underwear off. As they lay naked, Dolly was overcome by the feeling of their two bodies pressed together. The sensation was deeper than any she'd ever experienced. The heat from Tommy's body warmed her to her core.

When Tommy kissed her again, Dolly didn't even try to keep up. She kissed her back at her own speed. Tommy seemed fine with that. She slowed her tongue down and fueled the fire burning in Dolly.

Dolly rolled onto her back and looked up at Tommy. Her blue eyes were dark as the midnight sky, and Dolly felt herself falling into them. But how was that possible? She placed her palms down and felt the bedspread under her. So she was lying flat. Phew. She shook her head to shake off the falling feeling.

"Baby? What's wrong?"

"Nothing."

"Something. Now, what?"

"Just stoned I guess."

"I get that. Isn't it groovy?"

"Scary, too."

"Scary. How so?"

"Nothing." Dolly was too embarrassed to say what she was feeling.

"Nothing should be scary, baby. Just enjoy the feelings. Relax and go with them."

Tommy kissed down her chest and when her mouth closed over a nipple, she felt a heat wave wash over her. She could actually see the air move as Tommy sucked on her nipple. It was almost too much, but then Tommy closed her teeth lightly over it, and Dolly felt her clit stiffen. She pictured it in her mind's eye, pink and standing up. She put her hands on Tommy's shoulders and pushed her downward, urging her to suck her enlarged morsel.

Tommy laughed.

"Someone's in a hurry, huh?"

"Need you," Dolly managed.

Tommy licked every inch between Dolly's legs. Dolly closed her eyes and tried to focus, but she was on a cloud, floating above the bed, watching Tommy make love to her. She fought to bring herself back to the bed, but it wasn't easy. Floating was easy, and she was half tempted to stay up there.

Finally, Tommy broke through the haze and Dolly felt the need to come. Suddenly, she was back on the bed and Tommy was sucking her clit and she was teetering on the precipice. She kept her eyes closed and concentrated with all her might. At last, bright lights exploded behind her eyelids as she rode orgasm after orgasm.

"Hey, baby," Tommy said. "Are you with me?"

"That was out of sight," Dolly said.

"Good. I'm glad you enjoyed it."

"No, it was more."

"More than what?"

"More than spectacular."

"Right on."

"How does marijuana do that?" Dolly said.

"Do what?"

"Make things so unreal."

"I'm not sure what you mean? You mean like intensify everything?"

Dolly thought about everything she'd just experienced. She felt like a fool. There was no way she'd tell Tommy.

"Yeah," she said.

"Isn't it groovy? It makes everything better. Have you ever come that hard before?"

Dolly didn't have to think twice to answer the question.

"Never."

"Good."

Dolly wanted to make love to Tommy then. She knew it was her turn, and it was always such fun pleasing her. She just didn't know if she'd be able to focus enough to get Tommy off. She kissed her longingly, willing her tongue to run over and around Tommy's. She kissed down her body until she was between Tommy's legs.

She dipped her head to taste her and once again, the strangeness began. She could see the different flavors of Tommy. How was that possible? She started to float again, but forced herself to stay grounded.

"Baby, that feels so good," Tommy said from somewhere in the distance.

Dolly continued licking inside her, tasting red and green. It made no sense to her, but if Tommy was enjoying it, she wasn't going to stop. She moved her mouth to Tommy's clit, which tasted bright orange. She licked and sucked at it with severe perseverance. She needed to focus on just the clit. If she could do that, she could make Tommy come. She felt herself flying just outside her body. She let herself go and watched her sucking Tommy. It was a beautiful sight. Tommy's hand on the back of her head finally brought her back to reality. Tommy soon cried out and Dolly smiled, proud of herself.

"That was too fuckin' much," Tommy said. "Holy shit."

"Yeah? You liked?"

"Yeah. I did."

"Thanks."

"No," Tommy said. "Thank you."

They curled up in bed together and Dolly fell into a deep sleep in Tommy's arms.

Sometime in the middle of the night, they woke to the sounds of shouting and pots and pans rattling.

"Go home!" voices chanted. "Baby killers go home."

People yelled obscenities, and Dolly burrowed more deeply against Tommy, who pulled her close.

"Sh," Tommy said. "It's okay. No one will hurt you. They don't know you're here."

"But why are they here?"

"This is the closest motel to the pier. It's logical that navy personnel would stay here. But they're not after you as an individual. Stay here and soon they'll pass."

Dolly pulled her covers up over her breasts and leaned into Tommy.

"I'm scared."

"Don't be, baby. We make a lot of noise, but we're peaceful. How would we be any different from you if we engaged in violence?"

Dolly wanted to believe her, but it was hard. She was still stoned, so the logic escaped her. They heard a loud crash followed by the crowd cheering. Tommy pulled her shirt and jeans on and went to the window.

"A car in the parking lot's been turned over. The crowd is moving to another car. Wait. Do you hear that?"

Dolly heard sirens in the distance growing nearer.

Tommy stood at the window.

"They're leaving. They're running away in all different directions." She turned away from the window. "They're gone now. And it looks like the owners of the car are out there checking out the damage."

Dolly was shivering.

"Do you have some night clothes here?" Tommy asked.

"Why don't you just hold me?"

"I will," Tommy said. "But you need warmth right now in a big way. Here."

Tommy handed her some thick pajamas she pulled out of her suitcase. Dolly quickly dressed in the fluffy green pajamas and climbed back under the covers. Tommy sat on the edge of the bed.

"I thought you were going to hold me," Dolly said.

"Right." Tommy climbed into bed.

"What's going on?" Dolly asked. "What's on your mind?"

"Nothing."

"I don't believe that. Talk to me."

"We're not violent," Tommy said. "We're not. I swear."

"Was that your group? Did you see anybody you recognized?"

"It's dark out there, Dolly."

"That doesn't answer my question. And the parking lot is lit up, so it's not that dark."

"They all had bandanas around their faces. I couldn't recognize any of them."

"But you think it was your group, don't you?"

Tommy sat silently. Dolly would have paid good money to see what was going on in her mind. She sensed disappointment. Was Tommy their leader? Had they fallen to chaos without her for just a couple of days?

"I don't know," Tommy said finally. "I hope not. I really hope to God not."

"Are you their leader?"

"No. Yeah. Not really."

"Well, that certainly cleared things up." Dolly laughed.

"We don't have a real leader, you know? We're all a bunch of hippies. It's not like there's a president and board of directors or whatever."

"Of course not. But the others look to you, don't they?"

"Sure. I guess."

"Are you worried about being away from them for so long?"

"Hell no. They're adults. They're probably just hanging out and getting high. They may not even have noticed I'm gone. I think this was someone else."

The motel room was lit up with alternating red and blue lights.

"The cops might want to talk to you," Tommy said.

"I was in bed. I didn't see anything."

"Tell them that. Be honest. Tell them I was the one looking through the window."

"Are you sure?"

"Positive."

As if on cue, there was a knock on the door. Tommy answered it.

"Tommy Benton," the cop said. "I should have known I'd find you around this mess."

"I had nothing to do with it," Tommy said.

"Where you been, then?"

"Right here."

The cop looked over and saw Dolly sitting in bed. Dolly was humiliated having been caught like this with another woman. She was sure her face was purple as she fought back tears.

"Has she been here, ma'am?"

Dolly nodded.

"Did either of you see anything?"

"Tommy was at the window," Dolly felt like a traitor for saying it.

"Yeah? And what did you see, Benton? All your friends turning over a car?"

"It wasn't my group," Tommy said.

"How can you be so sure?"

"They wore bandanas over their faces. We never do that. And we're not violent."

The cop stared at Tommy for a long time.

"True. You're annoying as hell, but you're not violent. All right," he tipped his hat to Dolly. "Sorry to have bothered you, ma'am. Enjoy your night."

He left and Tommy closed the door. Dolly collapsed into a pillow and began to sob.

"What's up, baby?" Tommy rubbed her back.

"What if he'd asked my name? What if he found out I was in the navy?"

"But he didn't. Everything's cool. Just relax, baby."

Dolly's body was no longer racked with sobs, but she still cried.

"Do you want me to leave?" Tommy asked.

Dolly thought about it. Was that what she wanted? Everything could go back to normal for her. But did she want normal if that meant no Tommy?

"No," Dolly said. "I want you here with me."

"But the idea of me with you seems to upset you."

"I'm so confused. And my brain's still fuzzy from sleep and marijuana."

"Okay, well, let's just go to sleep and we'll talk about things in the morning," Tommy said.

"That sounds great."

They curled up and went back to sleep. The next morning, Dolly was up before Tommy. She waited for an hour, but when Tommy still didn't awaken, she decided to go for a walk. It turned out that the driveway of their motel was not the only place hit by the protesters the night before. There were cars overturned in several places. But the closer she got to the water, the less damage there was. She was able to walk on the shore and enjoy the cool ocean breeze. She let the morning air refresh her, and she was able to think about what she really wanted.

Liberty wouldn't last forever. That was her first thought, and it brought tears to her eyes. She swallowed hard as she thought of a future without Tommy. But certainly Tommy wasn't serious about a woman who believed in everything she fought so hard against. She would just enjoy these next few days and then go away with fond memories. But that wouldn't be easy. She was half tempted to go AWOL, but knew she'd never do it. She was a rule follower. And Tommy wasn't. But how did she feel about Tommy? Wasn't that what Tommy had questioned? How did she feel about being with her? Dolly knew the answer and turned to walk back to the motel.

CHAPTER SEVEN

Tommy stirred when she heard the door close. She propped herself up on an elbow and looked at Dolly.

"Where have you been?"

"I went for a walk."

Tommy sat up straighter.

"Are you serious? Didn't you learn from last night? That's not safe."

"I just walked to the water. No big deal."

"Still. I wish you wouldn't go out by yourself."

"I didn't want to wake you. You looked so peaceful sleeping there."

Tommy chose not to argue any more. Dolly was safe. That's what mattered. She lay back on her back and reached her arms out to Dolly.

"Come here," she said.

Dolly crossed the room to her. She lay down in her arms.

"Mm. That's nice," Tommy said. "Except you have too many clothes on."

"I could change that, I suppose."

"I wish you would."

Dolly stood and got undressed. She climbed under the covers with Tommy, who moaned in delight.

"You feel so good." Tommy felt the familiar stirring deep inside. "And you smell like fresh salt air."

"Take me, Tommy. I need you."

Tommy was happy to oblige. She'd never enjoyed a woman the way she'd enjoyed Dolly. It was a complete coupling when she made love to her. It was different, but wonderful. She could spend forever doing that.

She sucked on a full breast and slid her hand down her body to where her legs met. She found her slick clit and teased it gently before she moved her fingers inside her.

"More, Tommy. I need more."

Tommy slipped another finger inside her and moved in and out until Dolly reached down and rubbed her clit. Together, they took her to an orgasm that made her body quake.

Tommy held her until she was still.

"You okay?" she asked.

Dolly nodded.

"Good." She kissed the top of her head.

"I can't believe what you do to me," Dolly said.

"I love making love to you."

"I love it, too."

"So are you feeling better about us being together this morning?" Tommy said.

"I am. As a matter of fact, there's something I need to tell you."

"Do it. I'm all ears."

Dolly took a deep breath and her eyes teared up.

"Baby? Are you okay?"

"Yeah."

"So, what gives? Talk to me."

"I'm scared," Dolly said.

"I get that. Last night was rough."

"Not about that."

"Then what about?"

Dolly propped herself on an elbow and looked down at Tommy.

"Tommy?"

"Yeah?"

"You know how last night you asked about how I felt about being with you?"

"Yeah. And I'm asking again right now."

"So I thought about that on my walk this morning."

Tommy felt a cold fist of fear forming in her gut. She was sure she was about to be turned out. She should have expected it. But she had to hear it from Dolly. She swallowed hard.

"And what did you decide?" she almost whispered.

"I love you."

"You what?" Tommy was sure she'd misheard.

"Don't make me say it again."

Tommy looked up into Dolly's eyes. She was sure she'd see laughter or something there, but Dolly appeared to be dead serious. Which meant Tommy had to say something. What could she say? How did she feel? She knew the answer, but was she ready to say it out loud?

"Say something, Tommy." Tears were starting to leak from the corners of Dolly's eyes.

"I love you, too," Tommy said. "I love you so much."

"Are we crazy?" Dolly asked. "We hardly know each other."

"We're totally crazy," Tommy said.

"And we're diametrically opposed to each other in our beliefs."

"That we are. Can we make it work?"

"I want to," Dolly said.

"It won't be easy."

"But we can do it."

"I hope so."

Dolly kissed Tommy on her mouth, then kissed her way down her body. She was between her legs and Tommy felt her excitement grow. She loved the way Dolly loved her and couldn't wait to feel her tongue on her. She didn't have to wait long. Dolly licked her long and lovingly, and Tommy spread her legs to grant her greater access.

She closed her eyes and just felt. She felt Dolly's tongue on every inch of her as well as her warm breath. The combination left Tommy lightheaded. She felt her muscles tense up as she got close and then the orgasms hit and she was left a puddle of mass.

"You're amazing," she said.

"So are you."

Dolly curled into Tommy's arms again. Tommy felt so right with her there. As she held her, she pondered again their declaration of love for each other. No one ever felt like Dolly did. She had never wanted to spend every moment with someone like she did with Dolly. But did she really know her? And Dolly didn't know her. That was for sure. She knew the basics and what kind of person she was, but didn't know who she was. She was terrified as she realized she'd have to come clean about it. And soon.

"You still with me?" Dolly said.

"Sure. Why?"

"You just felt distant there."

"Nope. I'm here."

"Good, because this is where I want you."

"So what shall we do today?" Tommy said.

"You're the one who lives here. What do you want to do?"

"Well, I'm kind of a freak for museums. How do you feel about them?"

"I know there's a Naval museum I'd like to see. But how do you feel about that?"

Tommy was silent. That was the last place she'd want to see. Could she see it in good conscience? On the other hand, could she say no to Dolly?

"I take that as a no?" Dolly said.

"No. I'll go. But I can't promise to enjoy it."

"I can accept that. But the exhibits will be from wars before this one. Surely you don't think the other wars were wrong?"

"Korea was."

"I know a lot of people felt that way. What about World War II?"

"They bombed us. We had every right to retaliate."

"So you'll be okay with those exhibits?" Dolly said.

"I suppose I will."

"Good."

"But if we go see that, we also get to go see the Egyptian exhibit at the Museum of Natural History."

"Oh, that sounds great to me."

"Groovy. So let's get ready."

They took their shower together and Tommy took Dolly to yet another orgasm. After, they dressed and walked to Main Street where Tommy hailed a cab. She told him where she wanted to go.

"There was some trouble there last night, you know?" the cabbie said.

"Trouble?" Tommy said.

"Some kids broke some windows and shit like that. I think it's open today, but I can't promise."

"Thanks for letting us know. We'll check for ourselves."

They got to the museum to find windows boarded up.

"Do you suppose this was the same group?" Dolly said.

"No way of knowing."

"Did I tell you I saw lots of cars overturned on my walk this morning?"

"No, you didn't. I really wish you hadn't ventured off by yourself."

"We've had this talk. I made it safely." Dolly smiled at her.

"Okay. Let's see if this place is open."

They went to the main entrance and found it open for business. Tommy paid for both of them and let Dolly lead the way in. She immediately went to World War II.

"Shouldn't we start at the beginning?" Tommy said.

"We could, but I've always been obsessed with World War II."

"Okay, well this is your scene, so we'll do what you want."

Tommy stayed close with Dolly as she examined the pictures and artifacts. She had to admit, it was fascinating seeing the old equipment they used. Not that she knew what they used in present day. Except bombs. Bombs to kill innocent people. She could feel her anger inching up inside. She took a deep breath and closed her eyes.

"Tommy?" Dolly said. "Are you okay?"

"I'm hanging in there."

"We don't have to do this."

"Yes, we do. It's important to you, so it's important to me."

"But you're upset," Dolly said.

"No. I just need to stay focused on this stuff and not the current war."

The expression on Dolly's face changed.

"I'm sorry for what I do," she said.

"Come on. Let's sit," Tommy said. She led her to a bench. "You aren't sorry for what you do, so don't say that."

"I'm sorry for the barrier it puts up between us."

"How long have you wanted to be a nurse?"

"Since I was a very little girl. There was no doubt. I was even a candy striper in high school. I loved it so much. I couldn't wait to be a nurse."

"That's cool. Not many people are that sure. So, next question." She paused. "When did you decide to join the navy?"

"I knew I would as soon as I graduated. I told you, I've been obsessed with World War II since I was little. I thought it would have been so neat to be a WAVE."

"But you joined up even knowing you could go to war?"

"I didn't think they'd really send women out on battleships," Dolly said softly. "I thought I'd serve in a hospital stateside."

"So, you got more than you bargained for, huh?"

"Much."

They sat in silence for a few minutes, until Tommy decided she could handle the exhibit.

"Let's keep looking around," she said.

They spent another half hour at the World War II exhibit, then set off to find the Revolutionary War and make their way through the history of the navy in chronological order.

Tommy actually found it all very interesting. And she loved watching Dolly enjoying herself. Each era was more fascinating than the previous. Until they came to the Korean War exhibit. It was too similar to Vietnam, and Tommy felt the rage in her belly again.

"Excuse me," she said. She left the exhibit and went to sit in a small garden to cool her heels.

Dolly followed her out.

"I'm sorry. We should have skipped Korea," she said.

"No. It's part of your history. You deserve to see it. But I can't. The war was wrong, and I can't look at baby killing machines and be calm."

"They killed a lot of bad people, too, you know."

"So, you're defending them?"

"Tommy, let's not argue. We know this is one subject we don't agree on."

Tommy nodded. It was true. It was just something they'd have to agree to disagree on. But was it that simple? It was a pretty big sticking point. Could they get around it?

"So, about that Egyptian display," Dolly said.

"Oh, yeah. Let's go."

Tommy led the way down the street to the museum. It was fairly empty, given that it was the middle of the day on a Tuesday. They took their time examining the various sarcophagi and scrolls from ancient Egypt.

Dolly stayed close to Tommy, practically holding on to her. Tommy enjoyed the closeness, but thought it odd for Dolly to be so demonstrative in public.

"What's up?" Tommy asked.

"Nothing. Why?" Her voice shook slightly.

"You okay?"

Dolly took a deep breath.

"Dolly?"

"This stuff scares me. It creeps me out. There are dead people in these."

"That's what makes it so cool," Tommy said. "But you don't think so, huh? Okay, we'll cut the tour short."

They stepped out to the front steps of the museum, and Dolly took in some deep breaths.

"You gonna be okay?" Tommy said.

Dolly nodded.

"I'm sorry about that. You should have said something earlier."

"I didn't realize what the exhibit would be. And I didn't know I was so queasy about that stuff."

"You're okay now though?"

"Yeah."

Tommy looked thoughtfully at Dolly.

"So, I have to ask," she said.

"Yes?"

"If you're so squeamish, how can you be on a ship with kids coming back from the war? Surely there are dead kids there, too."

"I never see the dead ones," Dolly said. "And it kills me to see the wounded, but I work with the doctors to ease their pain and heal them."

"It's too bad there are any dismembered kids anyway. Off fighting a war we don't belong in."

"So you would have communism take over the free world?" Dolly said.

"That's just an excuse," Tommy said.

"It's not. The Viet Cong are trying to take over and make Vietnam a communist state."

"Even if they did, it's not our business."

"We're the most powerful nation in the world. If we don't fight against communism, who will? Besides, they have the Soviet Union and China helping them."

"They shouldn't be helping, either. The war, which is wrong anyway, but if there has to be a war, it should be between the people of the country. Without outside interference."

She could see Dolly's face flushing and knew this could easily turn into a full-fledged fight. That was the last thing she wanted.

"Okay, baby. That's enough of this talk. Let's talk about something else, a little more pleasant."

"You're right. How about lunch?"

"Now you're talking. I know a great deli in the neighborhood."

They walked to the deli and each ordered a sandwich. When they got to their table, Tommy took a huge bite out of her corned beef sandwich. She noticed Dolly had an odd expression on her face.

"What?" Tommy managed through a mouthful of food.

"Nothing. It's just that I thought hippies ate nothing but alfalfa sprouts and the like."

Tommy lifted her head up and laughed.

"That's a good one. I eat meat whenever I get a chance. Now, mind you, on the commune, there's not always an abundance of meat. And our meat is mostly fish that we catch. That's one of the reasons I come into town sometimes. To get my fill of meat."

Dolly was still looking at her questioningly.

"What?" Tommy said.

"You have money," Dolly said. "Obviously. Why don't you buy meat for everyone?"

"I don't have that much money," Tommy lied.

"That's too bad. I'm sure they'd appreciate it."

"Actually, a lot of them are vegetarians. They object to eating meat. So it works."

"Okay." She took a deep breath. "Are you ever going to tell me where you get your money? I still don't think being queen of the hippies could pay this well."

Tommy took a deep breath as well.

"Have you ever heard of Benton and Associates?"

Dolly's eyes grew wide.

"That cop last night called you Tommy Benton," she said.

"Yes, he did. I'm the only child of the famous Thomas Benton, land raper extraordinaire."

"Oh my God. That's almost impossible to believe. Talk about the apple falling way far away from the tree."

"That's for sure," Tommy said.

"How do they feel about your career choice?"

"Are you kidding? They wanted me to be a secretary or some such at my dad's firm. They sent me to college and didn't expect my eyes to be opened, I guess."

"You went to college? Where?"

"Berkeley."

"That's a radical school," Dolly said. "I'm surprised they let their little girl go there."

"They weren't thrilled with my choice. But, as Daddy's little girl, I got to go where I wanted."

"And how long did it take you to become the liberal opponent to everything you'd been raised to believe in?"

"A couple of years. I held on to my conservative beliefs for a while, even though they made me an outcast. But then I started thinking on my own instead of letting my father think for me. And things became so much clearer."

Dolly nodded, seeming to take it all in.

"How often do you see them?"

"I don't," Tommy said. "Father refuses to let me in his house until I come back around to his way of thinking."

"And yet you still have access to his money?"

"He couldn't cut me off completely. He still loves me. So, he supports me financially even though he won't accept me."

"That's really strange."

"I agree. Mother did her best to talk him out of it, but he was insistent. I'm still his little girl and he couldn't stand to see me penniless."

"So, what's it like?" Dolly asked. "To protest cutting down trees to build houses and developments, knowing your dad's behind them?"

"I try to think of the land rapers as nameless, faceless beings, but it can be hard sometimes."

"Do you ever run into your father at those protests?"

"Never. He's far too old and established to do any work on site anymore. I keep asking him to close his company. He's made his fortune. Why keep doing it? But he doesn't listen to me."

"It must break his heart every time he sees a picture of you in the paper."

"Maybe. I try not to think about it."

"What if he ever gets tired of it and cuts you off?" Dolly said.

"I doubt he will," Tommy said. "Okay. That's enough about my parents. Tell me about yours."

"There's not a lot to tell about mine. They're simple folks. They own a peach orchard and are well off, but not in the same vein as yours."

"Peaches? I love peaches. And I've heard Georgia peaches are the best."

"They are by far," Dolly said. "Especially the ones my father grows."

"Why is that?"

"I don't know, but the packing companies are always knocking on the door waiting for our peaches."

"Well, that's got to feel good. And how do your parents feel about you being in the navy?"

"Pretty much how you do."

"Ah, so they're smart people," Tommy said.

"Of course you'd think so." Dolly laughed. "They're proud I'm a nurse and don't openly criticize my choice of the navy, but they worry."

"And rightfully so."

"It's not like I actually see action, Tommy."

"But you're a sitting target on the ship out there."

"Tommy, I don't want to have this conversation again."

"I know. It's just that now it's more than you supporting the war. It's that you could be hurt. That kills me to think of, baby."

Dolly looked at her with tears in her eyes.

"I promise to keep myself safe."

"You'd better. That's my heart you're carrying with you."

Chapter Eight

After lunch, they walked through downtown window shopping. They'd pop into one store after another, looking at clothes or jewelry or knickknacks. Tommy was enjoying herself immensely. Any time with Dolly was precious.

They were in an antique shop and Dolly was like a little kid in a candy shop. She loved vintage clothing and all the other items on display. Tommy stood back and watched her. She couldn't wipe the smile off her face. She was having so much fun. It filled Tommy's heart with joy to see Dolly so happy.

She followed Dolly up to the counter by the cashier to look at the jewelry on display. Dolly gasped, and Tommy leaned closer to see what had drawn the intake of breath. She saw a lot of rings on display.

"Which one caught your fancy?" she asked.

"That one. Right there. The silver filigree ring. Isn't it beautiful?"

Tommy had to admit there was a certain charm to the old ring.

"May we see this one?" she said to the cashier.

"Certainly," the woman replied. She reached into the display cabinet and pulled out all the rings. "I wasn't sure which one you meant."

"That's fine," said Tommy. "She knows which one."

She took the ring and gently slipped it on Dolly's finger.

"It fits perfectly," she said.

"It's beautiful," Dolly said.

"It's yours."

"Oh, Tommy, I couldn't. It would be too much."

"Nothing's too much." She almost said "baby" but caught herself in time.

"Yes, it really is. I mean, it's fun to dream about things like this, but that's all they are. Dreams."

"Not true. I'm buying it for you. You love it. You want it. And who knows if you'll ever see it again? So, I'm buying it. Now, is there anything else you see that you want?"

Dolly laughed.

"Only one of everything. But I couldn't take it on the ship with me."

"Fine then." Tommy turned back to the cashier. "How much do I owe you?"

She wrote a check and they left the store, the ring firmly on Dolly's finger. When they were out of earshot of anyone else, Dolly leaned in close and whispered in Tommy's ear.

"I do so love you."

"I love you, too, baby."

"Thank you for the ring."

"It looks great on you. You needed it."

"Still, thank you."

"So, what's next on our agenda?"

"I say we head back to the motel. I could use a nap."

"Sounds good to me," Tommy said. She caught a cab and they went back to their room. As soon as they were inside, Dolly was in Tommy's arms.

"Let me show you how much I love and appreciate you," Dolly said.

"You don't have to, you know?" Tommy said.

Dolly looked sad.

"Don't you want me to?"

"More than anything. But I don't want you to feel obligated. I mean, if you just want to nap, that's fine with me."

"A nap is the last thing I need."

She unbuttoned Tommy's shirt and slid it down her arms and tossed it on a chair. She pulled her undershirt off and did the same. She bent to take a small nipple in her mouth, taking most of Tommy's breast with it. She sucked hard and Tommy couldn't help but moan at the sensation. She wanted Dolly to stay there all day. Just as she wanted Dolly between her legs. She just wanted Dolly.

She tangled her fingers in Dolly's hair and held her head there. Her own head was thrown back as she arched into Dolly's' mouth. Dolly continued to suck as she deftly unbuttoned and unzipped Tommy's pants. She released her grip on Tommy's breast so Tommy could step out of her jeans and underwear.

The two of them worked together to get Dolly naked, and when they were both without clothes, Dolly took Tommy's hand and sat her on the bed. Tommy reached for Dolly's breasts, but Dolly had other plans. She knelt between Tommy's legs and spread them wide.

Tommy felt Dolly's mouth on her and groaned. It was a guttural sound that came from the center of her being. She loved how Dolly loved her. She was skilled at pleasing her in a way no other woman had been. She knew just where to lick, just where to suck to keep Tommy begging for more. And beg Tommy did.

"Baby, that feels so good. Please don't stop."

Dolly teased her endlessly. She took her to the brink then backed off several times.

"No, baby. No. Please. Let me come," Tommy said.

Dolly finally took pity on her and sucked her clit until Tommy felt the orgasm creep up on her and crash over her.

Tommy lay there catching her breath. She was still dizzy from the force of her climax. Her legs felt like noodles. And all she wanted was to treat Dolly to the same experience.

She kissed Dolly hard on the mouth, tasting her own orgasm there. She was still light-headed, but was determined to please Dolly. She kneaded one of her plump breasts before taking her nipple in her mouth. Dolly moaned in pleasure, which urged Tommy on. She moved her hand down Dolly's belly and placed it between her legs. She lightly dragged it over her while still sucking on her nipple. Dolly placed her own hand over Tommy's and pressed it into her.

Tommy laughed, but slipped her fingers inside Dolly. She stroked her lightly at first and then with more pressure. She found that soft spot she knew Dolly liked so much and concentrated all her energy there.

It took very little time for Dolly to cry Tommy's name as her pussy crushed Tommy's fingers.

"Oh, my God. That was out of this world," Dolly said.

"Yeah it was."

"We're so good together."

"Yeah we are," Tommy said.

They dozed together, and when Tommy awoke, she noticed the sun was going down. She was also famished. She wanted to get up and get dressed, but didn't want to disturb Dolly. She needn't have worried. Dolly rolled over and wrapped her arms around Tommy.

"Are you awake?" Dolly said.

"Yeah. Are you?"

"Kind of."

Tommy laughed and kissed the top of Dolly's head.

"I was just thinking about dinner," Tommy said.

"How can you eat so much and stay so slim?"

"Just lucky, I guess."

"Okay, well, what do you want for dinner?"

"I want a thick rib eye with a baked potato," Tommy said.

"Sounds delicious, but I'm really not that hungry."

"I have something that can help with that. First, let me get you a glass of wine."

Tommy padded across the room, completely at ease in her nudity.

"I like this sight," said Dolly.

"Good," Tommy said. "Because you're going to be seeing a lot of it."

She poured Dolly a glass of wine and herself one of bourbon then walked back to the bed and handed Dolly hers. Dolly sat up in bed, but kept the sheet pulled up under her chin.

"Oh, no you don't," Tommy said. "I want to see those every minute that I can."

She gently peeled the sheet down to Dolly's waist. She dipped her fingers in her bourbon and coated one of Dolly's nipples. She bent and sucked it clean. She did the same with the next one. After that, she had to set her drink down and take Dolly once again.

It took barely rubbing Dolly's clit to get her off that time. She was primed and Tommy knew just how to touch her. Tommy reached across her to her nightstand and picked up her wine.

"Here you go," she said.

"Thank you."

Tommy sipped her drink and looked at Dolly.

"So, still not hungry?"

"Not overly so."

Tommy got out of bed and crossed the room. She reached into the pocket of her flannel shirt and withdrew the remainder of the joint they'd shared.

"Oh no, Tommy. I can't be seen in public stoned."

"What are the chances you see anybody from your ship?"

"That won't matter. I can't contain myself on marijuana."

"You'll be fine," Tommy said. She lit the joint and handed it to Dolly who eyed it suspiciously. "It won't hurt you."

Dolly finally took a hit. Not a long hit, but a hit. She handed it back to Tommy who took a long drag.

"Do you want any more?" Tommy said. "Remember how good you felt last night?"

"You're right. It was fun."

She took another drag and Tommy took it from her and set it down in the ashtray. Tommy sat back on the bed with her and they sipped their drinks.

"So, I know this great steak and seafood place. Do you like seafood?"

"I love it."

"Great. It's right on the waterfront. Sound good?"

"Sounds great."

"We can walk there from here," Tommy said.

"Right on. Let's go."

"Let's get dressed first." Tommy smiled.

"Oh yeah." Dolly fell backward on the bed, laughing so hard she was crying.

"You're so fucking sexy," Tommy said. She climbed on top of Dolly and kissed her, plunging her tongue deep in her mouth. She pressed her knee against Dolly and felt the wet heat radiating from within. She needed her again. She couldn't get enough of her.

Tommy put her hand between her knee and Dolly and used her knee to propel her fingers deeper and deeper with each thrust. Dolly was thrashing her head back and forth on her pillow, and Tommy finally gave up trying to kiss her.

"Oh dear God, Tommy," Dolly said.

"Do it, baby. Come for me."

"Oh God, yes. Yes. Now. Right now. Oh my God," Dolly cried out and closed her legs around Tommy's knee.

"You're so fucking sexy," Tommy repeated. She looked into Dolly's bloodshot eyes and saw a reflection of love in them. It almost made her weep for joy. Almost.

"I need a shower," Dolly said.

"I'll join you."

"Not a good idea."

Tommy laughed.

"Ah, short phrases again. Let me guess, your thoughts aren't coming out your mouth again?"

"Exactly."

"Well, you're going to need to focus hard when we're at the restaurant. Promise me you'll try?"

"Promise."

They took a shower together and once again, the nearness of a naked Dolly was too much for Tommy to stand. She watched the water drip over her figure and traced the drops with her fingers. She followed them to where her legs met and slid her finger over her clit.

"Oh God. Not again," Dolly said.

"Yes, again."

Tommy stroked her until she came for her, holding on to Tommy's shoulders to keep from slipping to the floor of the shower. They finished their shower and toweled each other off.

While they were getting dressed, Tommy felt the need to check in on Dolly.

"How you feeling, baby?"

"Okay."

"Just okay?"

Dolly giggled.

"I feel funny."

"So you're stoned. That's cool. But are you going to be able to hold it together?"

"Yeah. I just feel good."

"That's it. Focus on stringing sentences together."

"I can do this," she said slowly.

"You're so fucking cute."

"I'm glad you think so."

"I do, baby. I really do."

"I'm starving," Dolly said.

"Well, let's get dressed and we'll head over."

They walked out into the evening air and Tommy fought the urge to hold Dolly's hand. She kept forgetting they weren't on the commune where anything went. One thing about time spent with Dolly, it reaffirmed for her that the commune was the place for her. Although she'd enjoyed all the time she'd spent with her, she missed the freedom the commune afforded her.

The restaurant was several blocks from the motel, but the walk was nice. The salt air smelled refreshing and stung a little when it hit her face. They arrived at The Rusted Anchor to find the wait a half an hour long. They took their seats at the bar and Tommy ordered drinks for both of them.

"How you doin'?" Tommy said.

"Great. I like this place."

"Good," Tommy said.

"It feels like I'm in an old shipwreck."

"I think that's what they were going for."

"I can hear the waves crashing against the side of the boat."

"I think that's from outside on the beach," Tommy said.

"Not to me. To me it's here."

Tommy was glad she'd learned to speak stoned Dolly.

"Okay, baby. If you say so."

"No," Dolly said.

"No what?"

"No baby. Not here."

"Oh shit. I'm sorry. It won't happen again."

"Okay. Thanks."

Tommy sat back and relaxed as she sipped her bourbon. She looked around the dark restaurant. She didn't know what wood it was, but it was darkened and looked like it was very old. She loved this place. It made her feel comfortable.

She looked over at Dolly and watched as the color faded from her face.

"Oh shit," Dolly said.

CHAPTER NINE

W hat's wrong?" Tommy asked.
Dolly didn't answer, just stared off at the two men coming their way. Tommy turned and followed her gaze.

"Who are they?" She said.

"My commanding officer."

"Oh shit. It's cool. Be cool."

The men arrived at their table.

"Samson? Is that you?"

"Yes, sir, Captain."

"How's liberty treating you?"

"I'm having a great time," Dolly managed. "How are you?"

She felt Captain Finley's intense focus on her eyes. She knew they were bloodshot. She had to hold it together and not let him know she was stoned.

"Are you waiting for a table?" he said.

"Yes, sir."

"So are we. Do you mind if we join you?"

Dolly swallowed hard. She was fighting tears. But how could she explain that to her C.O.?

"Please do."

"And who is your lovely friend?" Captain Finley asked.

"This is Tommy," Dolly said, grateful to have his attention off her. "Tommy, this is Captain Finley, my commanding officer."

Tommy extended a hand.

"Nice to meet you, sir."

Dolly held her breath, waiting to see if Tommy would go off about the war. But she was playing it cool. She appreciated that.

"Nice to meet you, too. Now, what are you ladies drinking?"

"Red wine for me and Tommy drinks bourbon."

"Bourbon?" He raised his eyebrows. "That's quite a drink for a young lady such as yourself."

Dolly knew Tommy was using every ounce of self-control to keep her composure. She watched her bristle slightly and hoped Finley didn't notice.

"It's the first booze I ever tried," Tommy said. "I was hooked immediately."

"And just how old were you when you first tried booze?" Captain Finley said.

Tommy laughed.

"I think I'll just decide not to answer that question."

Captain Finley walked up to the bar and came back with their drinks.

"So, what have you been doing on liberty, Samson?"

Dolly fought hard to concentrate. She was starting to feel the same fog she'd felt the previous night. She just wanted to relax into it. But Finley was talking to her. She knew she'd have to form sentences. It wasn't going to be easy, but she tried.

"Mostly touristy things," she said.

"Like what?"

"We went to the zoo one day," she managed. "And to some museums another."

"Oh, that sounds nice. What kinds of museums?"

"We went to one about naval history."

"Fascinating. And good for you. It's important to know our history. I'm impressed, Samson."

"Thank you, sir."

"What did you see that interested you?" he said.

Dolly fought through the fog and struggled to stay focused. What had she seen? That should be easy to answer.

"The World War II exhibit."

"Ah, yes. Some of our most shining times. At least for the navy that survived Pearl Harbor."

"Yes, sir," Dolly said.

The hostess arrived and thankfully took them to their table. Dolly sat and couldn't decide whether to laugh or cry. She was so relieved to be away from her Captain Finley, but the whole ordeal had been too much. Tears streamed down her cheeks.

"Baby? What's wrong?" Tommy said.

"That was scary." Dolly wiped away tears. They threatened to come harder and faster, but she fought to keep them at a trickle.

"It's okay, Dolly. They can't even see us from where they're sitting. There's no need to worry anymore. You did fine. Relax, okay?"

Dolly nodded. She was just so relieved to have lived through that. She couldn't believe Captain Finley was at the same restaurant she was. And she was stoned! Suddenly, the tears changed to tears of laughter. She had been stoned in front of Captain Finley and had gotten away with it.

"Dolly? Try to hold it together," Tommy said.

"I can't. It was too precious."

Tommy stared at her, but soon joined in.

"See? It feels good to laugh, doesn't it?" Dolly said.

"Yes. But we look like we're stoned."

"We are."

"People don't need to know that," Tommy said.

"I'm sorry," Dolly said. "Not really, but I'll try to be."

"Try to be sorry?"

"Try not to act stoned."

"You're not making a lot of sense," Tommy said.

"That's okay," Dolly said. "Let's order."

Dolly was famished. She wanted one of everything on the menu.

"Oh my God. It all looks so good," she said.

"Of course. You've got the munchies. Order anything you'd like."

Dolly took a slice of bread and spread a generous amount of butter on it. She took a bite and swallowed it quickly.

"Oh my God, this bread is to die for."

"You're going to think anything tastes excellent at this point," Tommy said.

"Right on."

"Have you decided what you want for dinner?"

"Surf and turf."

Tommy laughed.

"Are you sure you'll be able to eat all that?" she said.

"Sure. No problem."

"I'm sure you think so now, but there's no way."

Dolly was bummed. She really wanted the surf and turf.

"But you said I could have whatever I wanted," she said.

"And you can. Oh, I'm not saying you can't have it. I'm just saying you'll never be able to eat that much, no matter how hungry you feel right now." Tommy smiled. "I'll get you whatever you want. I'd never deprive you."

"Great." Dolly smiled. "I'm excited. I've never had that before and I swear I could eat half a cow right now."

"Me, too," Tommy said. "Maybe I'll have the same."

The waitress came and they ordered. Tommy also asked for another basket of bread, since Dolly had emptied the first one.

"I kind of like feeling this way when I'm just allowed to feel," Dolly said.

"You mean when you don't have to hold it together in front of your C.O.?"

"Exactly."

"Well, good. Relax and enjoy the buzz now."

Dolly did as she was told. She let herself listen to the conversations going on around her, until they lost their meaning and simply became static in the background. Then she stared at Tommy. She focused on her rugged features, her soft hair that she kept in a braid down her back, and her hands. She loved Tommy's hands. Her fingers were long and talented. The thought made her blush.

"What?" Tommy said.

"What what?"

"You're blushing. Why?"

Dolly felt the heat on her cheeks but couldn't stop it. It only deepened. She couldn't tell Tommy what she'd been thinking. The idea was preposterous. She started laughing at the thought. She laughed harder and harder. Soon she could barely breathe.

"Are you okay?" Tommy laughed with her, then said quietly. "You seem like you've lost it. Can you bring it back together?"

Dolly heard Tommy's voice through the fog. It sounded distant. She was laughing, too. Everything was groovy, but Tommy sounded concerned, too. What did that mean?

"Huh?" Dolly said.

"Come back," Tommy said. "Here comes the waitress with our food."

"Okay." Dolly took a deep breath. "I can do this."

It wasn't easy. She wanted to bust out laughing again. Everything was funny. But she couldn't get them in trouble, so she held her breath and stared at the table.

"Here's yours, medium rare." The waitress set her dinner in front of her.

"Thank you," Dolly mumbled. She knew if she tried to say anything more, she'd start laughing like a hyena again. She could feel the laughter bubbling up inside her and fought to hold it together.

"And here's yours, well done," she said to Tommy.

When she walked off, Dolly exhaled. She giggled slightly.

"If you keep laughing," Tommy said, "you'll choke on your dinner."

"I know. I know," Dolly said. "I'm trying."

They ate their dinner in a relaxed silence. Dolly managed not to burst out laughing as she devoured the most delicious meal she'd ever had. The steak was cooked and seasoned perfectly, and the lobster was succulent. She finished every bite and sat back with a satisfied stomach.

"You look happy," Tommy said.

"Oh my God. That was delicious."

"Good. I'm glad you enjoyed it. I'm kind of surprised you ate the whole thing."

"You did, too," Dolly said.

"Yes, I did. And I don't have any regrets."

"Can we get dessert?"

"Are you serious?"

"I'm craving something sweet," Dolly said.

"If you're craving it, we shall have it."

They split a piece of chocolate mousse cake. Dolly thought it was the best cake she'd ever had. She had to force herself not to lick the plate.

Tommy paid the bill and they walked back to the motel. The cool sea breeze sobered Dolly somewhat, but not completely. She was able to simply enjoy the buzz without the crazy urge to giggle. She liked the buzz.

"I could get used to the buzz," she said.

"Yeah? It's nice isn't it?"

"It is. The uncontrollable urge to laugh isn't much fun in public, but the nice, easy buzz feels good."

"Good. I'm glad you're enjoying it."

They got to the motel and Tommy let them in. Dolly liked how chivalrous Tommy was. She always held the door open for her and did little things like that. Dolly really appreciated it.

"You're such a sweetheart," Dolly said.

"How so?"

"You just are. I really like you."

"So now you only like me?" Tommy teased her.

"No. I love you."

"Show me."

Dolly stepped into Tommy's arms and laced her arms around her neck. She moved closer and pulled Tommy down for a kiss.

"That was nice," Tommy said.

Nice? Dolly was tingling all over.

"It was better than nice."

"Yes, it was. And I want more."

Tommy pulled her back for another long, slow kiss that made Dolly's toes curl. Every nerve in her body was on alert. She felt Tommy trying to pull away, but wouldn't let her. She needed this kiss to never end.

But end it finally did, leaving Dolly breathless and yearning for more. She knew Tommy would give her much, much more. She sat on the bed and patted the spot next to her. Tommy sat beside her and held her hand. Dolly was amazed how much comfort she could get from that simple gesture. Everything Tommy did was just right.

"I love you so much," Dolly said.

"I love you, too."

Tommy kissed her again, and Dolly leaned backward until she was lying flat on her back. She spread her legs, begging Tommy to touch her, even through her clothes. Tommy kept on kissing her as she ran her hand all over Dolly's body, setting off sparks of electricity everywhere she touched.

"Let's get out of these clothes," Tommy said.

Dolly was happy to oblige. She was up and undressed in no time at all.

"Someone's in a hurry," Tommy said.

"I need you so bad."

"I need you, too, baby. And I'm going to have you."

Tommy pulled Dolly onto the bed and kissed her so hard Dolly thought surely her mouth would bruise. She kissed her back with every ounce of pent up passion she was feeling. She was getting wet. She could feel her clit swell. No one affected her the way Tommy did.

Once again, Dolly spread her legs for Tommy. She took Tommy's hand and placed it between her legs. She was still stoned, so feelings were magnified. She was a hormonal mess and needed relief soon. Relief only Tommy could give her.

She rubbed against Tommy's hand, reveling in the feeling.

"Do it, baby," Tommy said. "Do what you need."

Dolly was suddenly embarrassed, feeling wanton in her actions.

"I'm sorry," she said.

"Don't be. I love a woman who knows what she wants. Keep goin'. I'm here, baby. It's my hand, after all."

Dolly was too embarrassed to continue. She released her grip on Tommy's hand and rolled away.

"Still. I'll let you do what you want," she said.

"I just want you to feel good. That's all that matters to me."

"I do feel good, Tommy. I always feel good with you."

"Groovy. Now get over here and let me have my way with you."

Dolly moved next to Tommy again. She opened her legs and welcomed Tommy's hand again. This time she let Tommy do whatever she wanted, and what she wanted was clearly to please Dolly.

She felt Tommy over her, on her and in her. She arched her hips, moving along with Tommy. They fell into a familiar rhythm, and Dolly once again felt herself floating outside her body. It wasn't scary. It was rather nice. She loved watching Tommy make love to her. It was beautiful to behold.

Suddenly, she crashed back into her body as the pressure at her core built to a fever pitch. She closed her eyes and focused all her attention on that pressure, on the pulsating need she was feeling. Finally, the tension broke loose and she rode a series of orgasms, one right after another.

"Oh my God," she said when she caught her breath. "That was mind-blowing."

"Good, baby. I want always to blow your mind."

"You always do."

Dolly rolled over on top of Tommy.

"Do you understand how much I really do love you?" she said.

"I suppose here is where you show me again?"

"You'd better believe it."

Dolly kissed Tommy hard on her mouth. She kissed down her cheek to her neck, where she nibbled and sucked softly. She moved her mouth lower and took one of her nipples in her mouth. She lovingly ran her tongue over the tip of it as she sucked it deep. She moved her hand between Tommy's legs and felt how aroused she was.

She easily slid inside Tommy and stroked her deep.

"More, baby. Give me more."

"Are you sure?" Dolly wasn't very experienced when it came to sex, and the idea of slipping another finger inside Tommy scared her.

"Positive, baby. Give me more."

Dolly slid another finger in her and continued to thrust. Tommy moaned, which encouraged her to keep doing what she was. Tommy grabbed her wrist and held it tight while she plunged in and out. Dolly felt Tommy's insides tremble and knew she was close. She stepped up her speed and then Tommy's closed almost painfully around her fingers just as she cried out.

"That was intense," Tommy said.

"It really was. I've never experienced anything like that."

"Good. I like being the first for you. In some things anyway."

"I like it, too. You introduce me to all sorts of fun new things."

"Baby," Tommy said. "You ain't seen nothin' yet."

CHAPTER TEN

Tommy awoke the next morning, her need for Dolly as great as the night before. Dolly was still asleep, but moaned lightly when Tommy moved. Tommy smiled to herself as she thought of other moans she'd be hearing soon.

She carefully climbed between Dolly's legs, making sure she didn't wake her. Not yet. She would soon enough. She ran her hands over the soft flesh of Dolly's inner thighs. They were so silky smooth, and Tommy moved lower to rest her cheek on one thigh. Dolly stirred again, but quickly settled back to stillness. Tommy starcd at the beauty that was between Dolly's legs until she couldn't stand it any longer. She dipped her head to taste her.

Lovingly, she dragged her tongue over every inch. She reveled in the unique flavor that was Dolly. She wanted to please her, to take her to the next level, but she also just wanted to enjoy her, to taste her and savor her. So she slowly moved her tongue over the length of her, tasting her muskiness, her sweet and salty areas. She could have stayed there all day.

Dolly moved again and Tommy stopped, not sure she was ready for Dolly to wake up yet.

"Tommy?" Dolly said.

"Yeah, babe?"

"What are you doing?"

"What's it feel like?" Tommy said.

"I thought I was dreaming."

"Nope, it's real."

"Okay then," Dolly said, "Don't let me stop you."

Tommy laughed and went back to her feast. She licked and sucked with greater fervor now. Knowing Dolly was awake drove her desire to please her ahead of her own enjoyment of her. She moved her tongue as deep inside Dolly as it would go. She lapped at the satin walls and tasted the extra juices that were now pouring out.

She licked her way to Dolly's clit, which she sucked in between her lips. The morsel felt very slick and warm. She swore she could feel it pulsating.

Tommy was getting more aroused by the moment. Nothing turned her on more than making love to Dolly. Dolly was so responsive, so knowledgeable, yet inexperienced. She was the perfect sex mate. Tommy pushed any thoughts about Dolly leaving soon out of her mind and continued to please her.

Dolly had her hand on the back of Tommy's head, pressing her face against her. Tommy found it hard to breathe but never missed a beat. She ran her tongue over Dolly's clit and tasted the special flavor that resided there. She was getting dizzy with her own need as she worked harder and harder on Dolly until Dolly screamed loud enough to wake the dead as she came all over Tommy's face.

Tommy moved her tongue all over her own face, lapping up the remnants of Dolly's orgasm.

"You taste delicious," she said.

"Come here and share."

Tommy was happy to oblige and lay patiently as Dolly kissed all over her face.

"I love you," Tommy said.

"I love you, too."

"That's a groovy thing."

"Yes, it is."

Tommy pulled Dolly close and held her against her. She had hoped that would quell some of her desire, but the feel of Dolly's large breasts pressed into her made her clit feel like it could explode on its own. She sat there stroking Dolly's hair, trying to think of anything but her own need.

"You are so sweet to want to hold me," Dolly said.

"I love you."

"I know. But I can't let you hold me. Not yet. Not until I repay you."

Oh thank God, Tommy thought. Finally, she would get some relief.

Dolly sucked on one of Tommy's nipples, pulling most of her breast in her mouth as she did. Tommy groaned in pleasure. Her nipples were hardwired to her clit, and she felt the sucking like a jolt of electricity in her nerve center. She tangled her fingers in Dolly's hair, holding her in place. Dolly showed no inclination to move, though.

As she sucked, she ran her hand down Tommy's stomach and came to rest between her legs. Tommy spread her legs wider, silently pleading for Dolly to do more. But Dolly didn't seem to be in any hurry. She lightly dragged her hand over every surface down there, not paying particular attention to any one area.

"Please," Tommy whispered hoarsely. "Please, baby."

"What's the matter?" Dolly said. "You don't like to be teased?"

"I'm so horny for you right now. I may come without your help."

"Oh, no. What fun would that be for me?"

"Well, if you don't do something soon, I swear it'll happen."

"How's this?" Dolly asked as she slipped her fingers deep inside.

"Oh God, yes, baby. That's it. More though. Give me more."

Dolly obliged and Tommy felt full as Dolly fucked her. She arched her hips and met every thrust. Dolly felt amazing. Just when Tommy thought her head would explode from the pressure building inside her, Dolly rubbed her thumb on her clit and Tommy saw fireworks. They exploded behind her eyelids as one orgasm after another rolled over her.

"Sweet Jesus, that was amazing," she said.

"Yeah, it was. I thought you were going to break my fingers."

"Sorry about that."

"Oh, no. Don't apologize. It's an incredible feeling."

"So what do you want to do today?" Tommy asked when Dolly was nestled against her.

"You're the tour guide. I'd be happy doing this all day."

"Ah, yes. But we need to eat."

"True. I'm sure we can find a way to do that with each other."

She blushed even as she said the words, but Tommy just laughed.

"I do like the way you think," she said. She kissed her on the top of her head. "But seriously, what strikes your fancy?"

"What's left that we haven't done?"

"There's the amusement park, the aquarium…"

Tommy felt Dolly sag against her.

"What's wrong, baby?"

"Just thinking."

"About?"

"Liberty's going to be over in a couple of days."

"Oh shit," Tommy said. "Yeah, I suppose it is."

"I don't want to get back on that ship."

"I don't want you to. So don't do it. Stay here with me."

"I can't do that," Dolly said. "I can't go AWOL. I'd be arrested."

"Being arrested isn't that big of a deal."

"Have you ever been arrested?"

"Baby, I'm an activist. It comes with the territory."

"Well, I'd be disgraced."

"You're saying I should be ashamed of myself for having been arrested?"

"No," Dolly said. "I mean if I went AWOL. Not for getting arrested."

"Okay. I was about to be offended."

"Please don't."

"So, now that we're talking about it, when does liberty end?"

Dolly laughed.

"What's so funny?" Tommy said.

"We are. We've been living like this is going to last forever and we never once talked about when it would end."

Tommy didn't see the humor in it. The idea of it not lasting forever didn't sit well with her. Soon, she would be back at the commune and Dolly would be off fighting a war Tommy opposed with every ounce of her being.

"Why is that funny?" she said.

"It just seems like something we would have talked about in the beginning."

"Yeah, I guess so. I'm really not looking forward to it ending, you know?"

"Neither am I."

Tommy felt a warm trickle on her arm.

"Baby, don't cry."

"I'm going to miss you."

"I'll write you."

"I'll write you, too, but mail isn't dependable on a warship."

"No?"

"Not at all. Plus, it'll probably be censored."

"Typical of the US government," Tommy said.

"And then there would be the problem of explaining who I'm getting mail from. Everyone will be curious. I can't very well say my girlfriend."

"Tommy could be a guy. How would they know if you didn't tell them?"

"I suppose that's true. Still, I hate to lie."

"So what you're saying is you don't want me to write?" Tommy was feeling angrier by the second. "It feels like you're trying to throw monkey wrenches into this when I'm trying to make it work."

"I want to make it work, too, Tommy. Honest I do."

"You sure don't sound like it."

"Let's not fight, Tommy. We only have a couple more days together. Let's make them as pleasant as we can."

"Fine. But we need to be thinking about how to make it work. Because I'm not going to give up unless you tell me to. I mean it when I say I love you. I've never said those words before, so I don't mean them lightly. But if you don't feel the same, you seriously need to let me know."

"I do feel the same, Tommy. I do. I guess I just don't want to think about leaving and all it entails."

"Well, we need to. Not right this second, but obviously very soon. We need to figure it all out before you leave."

"I understand."

"Okay." Tommy kissed her. "Let's get in the shower."

They showered together and Tommy took Dolly to two more orgasms.

"You never stop," Dolly said.

"Why should I?"

"I guess that's a good question."

"Yep. Now dry off and get dressed or I'll have to have you again."

Dolly got a mischievous grin on her face and lay back on the bed.

"I'm warning you," Tommy said. "I'm not messin' around."

"I bet I could make you mess around."

"Oh shit, why do I try?" Tommy laughed. She climbed onto the bed with Dolly and kneaded a massive breast. She played with it until Dolly's breathing got labored, then Tommy sucked Dolly's nipple deep in her mouth. She flicked her tongue all over it. She felt the nub harden. She was driving herself wild with need, as well as Dolly.

She placed her other hand between Dolly's legs and stroked her clit until she cried out for her.

"Thank you," Dolly said. "I needed that."

"You haven't had enough yet this morning?" Tommy was surprised.

"I have, really. But then, somehow with you I always want more."

"That's very sweet of you to say."

"It's true."

"Well, let's get you dressed so you're not tempted anymore. I don't know about you, but I'm famished."

"Oh yeah. Food sounds good."

"Hey, baby," Tommy said.

"Yeah?"

"Let's smoke a little before we go out. It'll make the amusement park more fun. Trust me."

"I don't know. I don't do so well on marijuana."

"You do fine. And you won't have to face your C.O. or anything like that today. So let's smoke, relax, and have fun."

"Okay," Dolly said hesitantly.

"Relax, baby."

Dolly nodded and took the lit joint when Tommy handed it to her. She inhaled deeply and gave it back to Tommy. Tommy took a long hit and passed it back. Dolly took another deep drag and gave it back again.

"I'm going to take one more hit," Tommy said. "But you've had enough, okay?"

"Sounds good to me."

"All right." Tommy put the joint out and tucked it in the pocket of her flannel shirt. "Let's get some breakfast. I'm about starvin' to death."

"I want grease," Dolly said.

"Yeah. Hash browns and bacon."

"Now you're talkin'."

"I know just the place," Tommy said. She hailed a cab and they shot off through town until it stopped in front of what looked like a wall.

"Thanks." Tommy paid the driver and climbed out, then helped Dolly out.

"There's nothing here," Dolly said.

"Can't you smell it?"

"I can. Okay. I'm confused. I can smell it, but I don't see it."

"Come here. Look closely. You'll see the door."

Dolly peered at the wall.

"I still don't see it."

Tommy walked over to a stone door and pushed on it.

"Oh my God," Dolly said. "How do people ever find this place?"

"They just know about it. It's famous. And it's delicious. Now, come on."

The waitress approached them and Tommy held her breath as she spoke.

"Are you still serving breakfast?"

"Yes, we are," the waitress answered.

Tommy exhaled and Dolly just giggled. They took their menus and looked them over.

"Anything grab you?" Tommy asked.

"It all looks so good."

"It's all going to taste as good as it looks. Trust me."

"Fine. I'll make up my mind soon, I promise."

"No hurry," Tommy laughed, knowing Dolly was feeling a little fuzzy in the brain. "Take your time and get something you really want."

The waitress came by and they placed their orders.

"How you feelin'?" Tommy said.

"Good. Really mellow."

"Groovy. That's what I like to hear."

"I don't have the urge to giggle right now."

"Far out. It can hit you different every time. Maybe this will just be a gentle buzz for you."

"I sure hope so."

The waitress brought their drinks and Dolly took a sip through her straw. She burst out laughing, with Coca-Cola shooting through her nose.

"What is it?" Tommy turned in her seat to see what Dolly had found so funny. She didn't see anything and Dolly showed no signs of being able to talk. So Tommy decided it didn't matter what Dolly had found so funny. She laughed at Dolly, which only made Dolly laugh more, which, in turn, made Tommy laugh harder.

This went on for several minutes until the waitress brought their food. Tommy took a deep breath and tried to gain control of herself. She looked at Dolly and started laughing again.

"Stop it," Dolly said.

"Me stop it? What about you?"

"No. Stop looking at me. You make me laugh."

"But I want to look at you."

"But you can't."

Tommy took another breath and made herself stare at her plate. Slowly but surely, she heard Dolly's giggles stop. She chanced a glance in her direction and Dolly nodded.

"I'm okay now, I think," Dolly said.

"Good. Although it sure felt good to laugh. I haven't laughed like that in a very long time. So, thank you."

"My pleasure. Now let's eat."

They finished their breakfast and Dolly sat back in her seat.

"That was delicious," she said.

"Yeah, it was."

"Now I want to curl up and take a nap."

"Oh no, you don't," Tommy said. "We have an amusement park to get to."

"That's right. Maybe I'll sleep on one of the rides."

"Or not. Come on. Let's get out of here."

They paid, left the restaurant, and caught a cab to the amusement park which was on a pier out over the ocean. It was breezy but not cold. The sun shone bright. It was a beautiful day.

"Where to first?" Tommy said.

"Oh my God. I have no idea. Everything looks like so much fun."

"Well, I'm up for anything from the Tunnel of Love to the Cyclone, so you make the call."

"Let's go on the Tilt-o-Whirl. I bet seeing everything spin will be beautiful right now."

"Even though we just ate? I don't want you throwing up on me." Tommy laughed.

"I won't. I promise."

They went on the ride and Tommy closed her eyes and just listened to Dolly's delighted giggles. Being stoned herself, she was thoroughly enjoying the twisting and turning. She felt her mind spinning with each rotation. It was a trip and she was wishing it would never end.

When the ride finally slowed to a stop, Tommy stepped out on unsteady feet and helped Dolly off.

"That was so much fun," Dolly said. "Let's do it again."

"There are other rides, too, you know. Some similar."

"And we have all day to go on them. Let's do this one again."

They got in the short line and were soon spinning again. Tommy kept her eyes open this time and watched everything pass by in a blur. She watched the colors separate and then come together. She wished briefly that she'd dropped some acid that morning, but she didn't have any, and she figured that would probably have been too much for Dolly.

When the ride stopped and they wandered through the park watching people and contemplating what to ride next, Dolly surprised Tommy with a question.

"Do you miss the commune?" she said.

Tommy stopped, the question having caught her completely off guard. She had to think for a moment.

"I miss my friends, sure. But it's only been a few days."

"I know, but it seems like we've been together forever."

"It does. I know what you mean. But I'll be back on the commune soon."

"Too soon."

"Yeah."

"I just wondered," Dolly said. "You don't talk much about it, which is weird."

"Come on now. You don't want to hear about a bunch of hippies who hate everything you stand for. So, why would I talk about it with you?"

"How did we ever manage to get together?"

"You were too charming after you bought me that drink. I knew then I could spend forever talking to you," Tommy said.

"You say the sweetest things."

"Well, it's true."

"Well, thank you."

Chapter Eleven

Dolly convinced Tommy to go on the Octopus, another twisting, turning ride that they were elevated for. So, ten feet off the ground, they spun, and once again, Tommy watched the delight on Dolly's face. They rode the Octopus several more times before Tommy pleaded motion sickness.

"Seriously? You're motion sick?" Dolly said.

"Well, maybe not really, but I am tired of that ride. We can come back to it later."

"That's fair. It's just that the spinning and twisting make me feel really good. I can't really explain it. The colors blur and are beautiful. The ride moves quickly while my brain moves slowly and the contrast is amazing."

"I get what you're saying. I'm feeling it, too. I would just like to do something else for a while."

They found their way to the midway where Tommy won a giant teddy bear for Dolly. Dolly hugged her tightly for just a moment. She realized how it must look and quickly pulled away.

"What's wrong?" Tommy said.

"I can't hug you like that in public," Dolly said. "What was I thinking?"

She could feel the tears welling in her eyes. What if someone had seen them? What if someone from the ship happened by right then? She felt nauseous.

"Don't cry," Tommy said. "I won you a toy and you hugged me. It's totally fine. People hug all the time. Relax."

Tommy reached out to pat Dolly's shoulder, but Dolly pulled away.

"Please don't touch me. Not here."

"Are you going to be okay?" Tommy said.

"Huh? Yeah. Let me just get it together. You're right, of course, it wasn't a big deal."

"Pot can make you paranoid," Tommy said quietly. "That could explain what you're feeling."

"I'm sure that's it."

"Come on. Let's get something to drink."

"Do they sell drinks here?"

"I was thinking of a soda, but if you want some wine, we can go to the beer garden. I'm sure they have wine there."

"But they probably won't have bourbon for you," Dolly said.

"That's okay. I can have a beer."

They made their way to the beer garden, got their drinks, and sat at a table in the sun.

"What a beautiful day," Dolly said.

"Made more beautiful because I'm spending it with you."

Dolly felt the blush start at the base of her neck and creep its way up.

"You're so cute when you blush," Tommy said.

"You're just going to make me blush more."

"Oh, well."

Dolly laughed. It was so easy to be around Tommy. The past few days had been heaven. She didn't want to see them come to an end, but knew they had to. She had to report back to the ship in two days. And what would happen then? Seriously, could they make it work?

"Whatcha thinkin'? Tommy said.

"Nothing. Just enjoying the day."

"Good. I want you to have a great time today. We've got lots more to do here."

"This wine is adding to the affects and making me very mellow," Dolly said.

"Not too mellow, I hope. We still have lots to do."

"No, not too mellow, just a nice peaceful feeling. I'll still want to go on rides and such."

"Can we do the Tunnel of Love next?" Tommy said.

"I don't know. Two women on that ride? It'll look suspicious."

She could see the frustration on Tommy's face. Her blue eyes darkened and she felt sure she'd upset her.

"You're still being paranoid," Tommy finally said. "You need to trust me."

"I do trust you, but you need to honor my concerns. What if I see someone I know?"

"Fair enough," Tommy said, but Dolly knew she wasn't happy.

"Do you like roller coasters?" Dolly said.

"I love them. You sure like motion rides, don't you?"

"I never thought about it, but I guess I do. And especially now. Everything just feels so much more magnified."

"I get that. I'm with you there. Oh. You know what would be fun? The haunted house."

"Oh yeah. Let's go there now."

The line for the ride was long, and Dolly found herself lost in her thoughts. She wondered what the story was behind the others waiting. There were regular looking people there as well as hippies, with their long, braided hair and leather vests. She pondered what they would do if they knew she and Tommy were lovers. She didn't think she looked like a lesbian, but was pretty certain Tommy did. But then, what did a lesbian actually look like? She supposed people thought most of them looked like men, but she knew better. Still, Tommy was masculine enough to draw attention to herself. Dolly questioned whether being seen with her the past few days had been such a good idea.

"Hey there," Tommy said. "Are you with me?"

"Sorry. What were you saying?"

"I was just asking how scared these rides make you. You're not going to have nightmares or anything, are you?"

"Oh no. I find them amusing, really. They make me laugh."

"Good. Just checking."

Finally, it was their turn to get on the ride. They climbed into the car and were locked in for the ride. Dolly loved the different colors on the old tapestries and thought the antique furniture would be wonderful to have. She had just settled in when an apparition popped out at them from behind a mirror. Dolly screamed and grabbed hold of Tommy. She relaxed against her and felt the familiar comfort of Tommy's arms around her.

Suddenly, she came to her senses and sat up, putting some distance between herself and Tommy.

"What gives?" Tommy said.

"Nothing."

"Something. You jumped away from me as if I was the ghost."

"I just felt foolish," Dolly lied. "I shouldn't jump so much. It's just a silly ride."

"Okay," Tommy said. "If you say so."

Dolly relaxed and actually began to dig the green specters floating around her. She allowed herself to be mellow and completely enjoy the sensation of being stoned. She thought about Tommy telling her marijuana could make her paranoid. Even so, she was worried today. Maybe it was the marijuana, maybe not. But nothing changed how she felt. She was terrified that she and Tommy stuck out like sore thumbs.

When the ride ended, Dolly mustered up all her courage.

"Do you mind if we call it a day?" she said.

"What? We haven't even had lunch yet. Why do you want to leave? Aren't you having fun?"

"I am…"

"But?"

"But, I feel like people look at us and know we're lesbians."

"How is that even possible? We're just a couple of young kids playing hooky and hanging out at an amusement park. No one would ever think you were a lesbian anyway."

"You did."

"That's because I'm one. I meant straight people."

"I don't know, Tommy."

"Look, if you're not comfortable, we can leave. But you've been fine the past couple of days, so I'm telling you it's the pot that's making you paranoid. You should be able to reason with yourself."

"I've tried. But it's not that simple. I can't turn off this fear burning in my stomach just because you say it's because I'm stoned."

"Let's get you some food. Maybe that'll take the edge off."

"Fine. I'm willing to try."

They went back to the beer garden and ordered burgers and fries. Dolly also had another glass of wine and Tommy ordered a beer. They sat quietly while they waited for their food. Tommy finally spoke.

"So, what's on your mind now?"

"Nothing. Just relaxing and soaking up this lovely sunshine."

"You sure?"

"Yeah. I can feel the sun entering each of my pores. It's an amazing feeling."

"Right on. I love feeling nature."

"I know what you mean. It's really groovy."

"Now you're talkin'," Tommy said.

Dolly laughed. She realized she was using Tommy's vernacular. It felt good. Tommy was a good person. Dolly knew that. She just questioned how bright it was to be seen hanging out with her.

The waiter arrived with two Monster Burgers and Dolly took a huge bite.

"Oh, my God. This is the best burger I've ever had!"

"Yep. Guaranteed to cure a hangover or whatever else ails you."

Tommy looked pointedly at Dolly, her comment not lost on her. The burger should make all of her concerns dissipate? That's what Tommy said. Dolly simply decided to enjoy her lunch and deal with any other issues as they came up.

She devoured the burger and felt more in control of her emotions. Suddenly, the idea of being seen with Tommy wasn't the end of the world. The idea of the Tunnel of Love was still too much, but just spending a day with Tommy felt the same as any other day. It must have been the marijuana, she reasoned.

"So, you ready for that roller coaster?" Tommy said.

"You bet."

They had to wait in yet another long line, but this time Dolly didn't worry what people were thinking about her and Tommy. And if they did think things, who cared? She didn't know anybody there, anyway. Unless she saw someone from the ship. But if she could handle having drinks with Tommy and Captain Finley, surely she could handle bumping in to anyone else.

The line seemed to be taking forever.

"We should have done another ride. This one is taking too long," Dolly said.

"But this is the one you want to go on. The wait can't be forever."

Dolly was struck yet again at how sincerely caring Tommy was. She would do whatever was in her power to see that all Dolly's wants were met. How had Dolly lucked out? How could she have known that one drink in a bar would have led to this? She couldn't have known, obviously, but she was so grateful things had worked out so far. And after tomorrow? She wouldn't let herself think about that. Not yet.

It was finally their turn. Dolly braced herself as she was buckled in. Sometimes roller coasters could be scarier than they appeared. She wanted to be ready for whatever it brought. The slow climb to the top only added to the apprehension. Her stomach was in knots by the time they reached the top of the first hill. And then they sped downward, around one corner and back the other way around another. It was exhilarating. The speed, the fresh air, it all made her feel alive.

And then there were the colors; the beautiful blending of colors as they sped past. It was as though God himself had left his palette out for them to see. She was mesmerized by the scenery. It was the most amazing sight she'd ever seen. She said a silent prayer, thanking whatever God there may be for introducing her to marijuana. She giggled out loud and threw her hands in the air, thoroughly enjoying herself.

Tommy looked over at her, a questioning look in her eyes. Dolly answered with a smile and a squeal. Tommy's face burst into a huge smile, and they laughed together as the roller coaster wove its way around the track.

Dolly got off the ride with unsteady legs but a steady heart. She was as happy as she had been the past few days. She loved Tommy. She loved being with her and doing things with her. She was struck yet again at how Tommy had indulged Dolly's every whim that day. Dolly felt it only fair to reciprocate.

"Why don't we go on the Tunnel of Love?" she said.

"Are you serious?"

"I am. Why not?"

"Fine. Let's do it."

The line for that ride wasn't as long and they simply had to wait for the previous riders to exit the ride before they got on.

"Oh, shit," Dolly said.

"What?"

"Lieutenant Martinez," she said. "He's on the ship with me and just got off the ride. I hope he didn't see me."

"Maybe he'll think I'm a dude with long hair," Tommy said.

"Oh, God. I hope so. He's gone now. Oh wow, Tommy. That was too close."

"It really was. I'm sorry. I should have listened to you and not gone on this ride."

"I made the decision," Dolly said. "It was up to me and I chose to go on it."

Dolly realized they were holding up the line and turned to climb into one of the little boats. Tommy had to help her, as her legs were shaking, but she got in and sat down. Tommy sat next to her. Dolly could feel her warmth radiating from her, even without her touch. But she wanted her touch. She craved it. She made up her mind this would be the last ride of the day. She wanted to go back to the motel. She needed some private time with Tommy. She relaxed and enjoyed the ride, having convinced herself that Martinez hadn't seen her.

The ride ended and Tommy stretched. Dolly took in that lean, lithe body and had to fight from wrapping her arms around her right there. She knew better, of course, but the temptation was still strong.

"So, where to now?" Tommy said.

"Back to the motel."

"Already? It's still early. There's still lots to do here."

"But there's lots to do at the motel, too." She hoped her look would convey her meaning.

"There is? Oh. There is," A slow smile spread across Tommy's face. "Still, we don't have to leave right now, do we?"

"We don't *have* to, but I'd sure like to."

"Right on. I get your drift. Let's boogie."

Dolly laughed out loud.

"What's so funny?" Tommy said.

"You're just such a hippie."

"How so?"

"Your choice of language is so different from mine. Not that that's a bad thing. It's just different."

"Different is good. It's what makes the world go round."

"I like that," Dolly said.

They arrived back at the motel and Dolly immediately stripped out of her clothes.

"Whoa, sister. Easy does it," Tommy said.

"I want you, Tommy. I want you with every ounce of my being. I can't wait another moment. I need you now."

Tommy smiled at her with a twinkle in her eye.

"I love your body," she said.

"And it loves you."

Dolly crossed over to the bed and lay on it while Tommy hurriedly undressed. She liked to watch Tommy undress, uncovering an inch or two of flesh with each movement. And Dolly couldn't wait to feel that flesh against hers.

Tommy was finally in bed with her and Dolly wrapped her arms and legs around her, pulling her close, needing that contact.

"Oh, God, Tommy. I can't stand to be away from your body."

"I wish we didn't have to hide our love in public," Tommy said. "I'd love to have my arm around you or hold your hand wherever we went."

"Not in this lifetime, I'm afraid."

"I don't know. I think free love is the first step."

"Maybe, but that's only practiced by a few, and they're on the fringes of society."

"You'd be surprised. I bet more mainstream women are lesbians than you'd imagine."

"Again, maybe, but they'll keep that part of themselves private. They won't show their love for all to see."

"I don't know," Tommy said.

"At any rate," Dolly said, "I'm tired of talking. Make love to me."

"Gladly."

Tommy kissed Dolly passionately, hard enough to convey her frustration with the limitations on their love. Dolly kissed her back with the same fervor, feeling Tommy's frustrations and sharing her own. As their tongues danced, Dolly felt the familiar pulsing at her center. She was already ready for Tommy. Of course, when was she not? And knowing that Tommy could take her to places she'd never been only caused more moisture to flow.

As they kissed, Tommy moved her hand down to cup one full breast. She kneaded it slowly yet meaningfully, coaxing Dolly's nipple to attention. She bent her head and sucked on her nipple while she worked her hand between Dolly's legs.

Dolly spread her legs and reveled in the feelings Tommy was creating. She could feel her clit swelling by the second, begging to be touched, but Tommy instead plunged her fingers inside. Dolly arched her hips to meet each thrust, moving them in circles to make Tommy touch all over inside her. She loved it when Tommy fucked her like this. It felt so carnal, so animalistic. She tried to hold out, but couldn't. She felt herself clamping over Tommy's fingers as her first few orgasms cascaded over her. She lay back to catch her breath, but Tommy clearly had other ideas.

Tommy slid her fingers out from inside Dolly and moved them to her clit, which she rubbed hard and fast. Dolly dug her fingernails into Tommy's back. Tommy slowed down and eased up on the pressure.

"Huh?" Dolly said. "Why did you stop?"

"I want to drag it out a little, let you enjoy it longer."

"I don't need to enjoy it longer. I just need to come. Please, Tommy."

Tommy went back to rubbing fast and hard again, and Dolly felt the familiar dizziness as her head seemed to spin with myriad feelings. Finally, Dolly focused all her energy on Tommy's fingers and her clit and she felt the wall break as one climax after another poured over her.

Chapter Twelve

It took Dolly no time to regain her strength, and with it, her desire to please Tommy. She loved everything about Tommy, from her sinewy body to her thick, full hair, to her unique flavor. There was nothing not to like. She was the full package, the real deal. And she was Dolly's.

Dolly kissed her hard on her mouth, moving her tongue inside with an authority usually foreign to her. She needed to convey to Tommy how much she meant to her, how much her very existence enlightened Dolly's world. Dolly rolled on top of Tommy and ground into her, using every method possible to let Tommy know she was desired.

"My baby's ready to love me up, huh?" Tommy said.

"Oh God, yes. I want to have you every which way I can."

"Far be it from me to argue with that."

"Good. What do you want, Tommy? Tell me what your deepest, darkest desire is so I can fulfill it for you."

Tommy lay quiet for a moment before she replied.

"Just to have you, baby. That's it. That's all I need is to have you with me."

Dolly wasn't sure she believed her. A woman as worldly as Tommy? Surely she had fantasies beyond what Dolly could think of.

"Are you sure? Don't be shy. You're not going to shock me. Be honest. Tell me your fantasies."

"Baby, believe me, twisted sex and fancy fantasies are nothing compared to true, honest loving with the one you love. And you're the one I love and all I want is for you to make love to me."

"Okay, because that is exactly what I'm going to do."

She kissed her again and brought her knee up to her center. It never ceased to amaze her how aroused Tommy got for her. She loved her so much and it blew her mind that Tommy felt the same way.

Dolly made her way down Tommy's body, stopping to suck on a nipple as she did. She moved her hand between Tommy's legs and stroked her swollen clit. She loved how slick it was, how warm and wet Tommy was. She had to taste her.

She moved her hand up to Tommy's nipple. She coated it in her juices and sucked it harder. She finally released her grip on it and replaced her mouth with her fingers. She tugged and twisted the nipple as she kissed lower and left a trail down Tommy's stomach. She knew she was teasing Tommy by going so slowly, but she was teasing herself, as well. She needed to taste her, to devour her essence, but she was making herself wait. She licked Tommy's belly button, enjoying the feel of it against her tongue. When she could stand it no more, she slid between Tommy's legs.

She sucked on Tommy's clit while her fingers continued to play with her nipple. She felt Tommy's hand on the back of her head and flicked her tongue over her clit.

"Oh yeah, baby. That's what I need," Tommy said.

Dolly sucked harder on her clit as she licked all the juices off it.

"Oh God, yes. That feels so good."

Dolly loved pleasing Tommy. It aroused her, to be sure, but there was more to it. So much more. It gave her a sense of purpose, a reason for being. Loving Tommy was what she was made to do. Regardless of anything else in her life, she knew this to be true.

She continued her focus on Tommy's clit until Tommy finally arched into her, then collapsed onto the bed, spent.

"Baby, you're amazing," Tommy said. "You sure know what you're doing."

"It's easy. I just follow your lead. Your body lets me know what you want and when you want it. Isn't that what making love is all about?"

"I suppose it is. Now get up here and let me cuddle with you."

Dolly was happy to move into Tommy's arms. She felt them encircle her and felt safe and warm.

"I don't know about you," Tommy said. "But I'm famished again."

"I just ate," Dolly said, then blushed.

Tommy laughed.

"That was very clever. And just a touch crude."

"I'm sorry."

"Don't be. Nothing wrong with a touch of crudeness on occasion. It's not like you walk around hocking loogies or scratching your pussy in public."

Dolly laughed out loud.

"Of course not."

"Then don't worry about making off-color jokes in the bedroom with me, okay?"

"Okay."

She snuggled closer, absorbing Tommy's warmth. She ran her hand over Tommy's body just to assure herself that she was really there and that this was really real. Sometimes it seemed like the past few days had been a dream. But it wasn't. Tommy was real.

"So about that dinner situation?" Tommy said.

"We'll need to shower. Then, what are you in the mood for?"

"I don't know. It's hard now to think about food because I'm thinking about showering with you."

"You're incorrigible."

"Thank you. And you're foxy as hell and I can't get enough of you."

"That's mighty nice of you to say."

"It's true."

Tommy rolled over on top of Dolly again and kissed her.

"You taste like me," she said.

"I hope that's okay," Dolly said.

"Yes, it is." Tommy ran her tongue all over the inside of Dolly's mouth, and Dolly felt the instant moisture between her legs. Tommy was so damned sexy and so damned talented. It took no time at all before she was dripping in anticipation.

Tommy lightly ran her hand down Dolly's body and played her like a fine musical instrument. Dolly was useless to try to protest. Not that she'd want to. The idea that Tommy wanted her and only her was heady indeed. She relaxed and let Tommy have her way with her.

Tommy added a little more pressure to her touches, leaving no doubt that she and Dolly were on the same page. There was no mistaking the passion in Tommy's touch. When she slipped her hand between Dolly's legs, Dolly was throbbing.

"You're killing me," Dolly said. "Just take me, for God's sake."

"Patience, my love. All in due time."

"It is time. Please."

"Sh. Just relax."

"I can't. I think I'm about to explode."

"Good," Tommy said. "I plan to help you do just that."

Tommy moved her fingers inside Dolly to stroke her special place and Dolly clawed her back as she screamed. Tommy didn't stop, though, and Dolly cried out over and over again, until she lay spent on the bed.

"Holy shit," Dolly said. "I didn't know it was possible to have that many orgasms at one time."

"Anything's possible when you're in love," Tommy said.

"Aw. That was so sweet. You really do love me, don't you?"

"I sure do. I don't know why, but I do."

"Well now, that wasn't so sweet." Dolly laughed.

"You know what I mean. I should hate you and all you stand for. And sure, you're beautiful, which was enough for one night, but you're compassionate, intelligent, and beautiful. That's a winning combination for me. I love how smart you are. And while I don't like that your compassion is directed toward baby killers, I still dig your ability to be compassionate. So, yeah, I guess I do know why I love you, even though I know why I shouldn't."

"You were doin' great there until the last few words."

"Sorry. I just had to say them."

"Tommy, I'm glad you find those wonderful traits in me. I think you're pretty far out, too. You're good-looking, smart, and worldly. I like those traits. But the fact that you're worldly means you have very strong opinions of what's happening in the world. And those opinions don't necessarily coincide with mine."

"No, they don't." Tommy pulled Dolly close.

"I'm scared."

"Don't be. We'll make it."

"I hope so. I've never felt like this before, Tommy."

"Neither have I, baby."

"It's overwhelming."

"It is, but we'll be fine. Trust me."

"Okay. I will."

"Now, how about some food?" Tommy said.

"That sounds good. I'm ravenous."

Dolly got out of bed and pulled Tommy with her. They took a shower where Tommy pleased Dolly yet again.

"I didn't think I had another orgasm in me," Dolly said as she toweled off.

"I knew you did. I could see it in your eyes."

"You could, huh?" Dolly laughed.

"Yep."

"That's good to know. I didn't know that showed in my eyes. I'll have to be careful. Do you suppose a stranger might read that?"

"Okay, funny girl. That's enough. Just get dressed and let's get out of here. I know a great little French bistro I want to take you to."

"Oh, that sounds delicious. I'm almost ready."

They finished dressing and headed out. The bistro was quite charming with its arched entranceway and latticework fence.

"How do you find these places?" Dolly said.

"From exploring. I figure since I chose this place to live, I should look around and get to know it."

"And since money is no object for you…"

"Exactly."

"Do you ever bring people from the commune with you?"

"You saw us at the club that night. That's about it, though. I don't take them to restaurants or anything like that very often for a couple of reasons. First, I don't want them to know how much money I have. Secondly, sometimes I just need to get away. That's usually when I explore, when I need to get away and have some quiet time. But I do bring them with me once in a while."

"Why do you do it, Tommy? Why not buy a place and settle down?"

"You mean give up my activism? Then what would I do? It's what I live for, Dolly. It's my passion. Imagine if I asked you to quit caring for people."

"Okay, but at least live comfortably. That I don't understand."

"I never know how long I'll be in one place. I move around. Not like every day or anything, but after a while, it's time to move on."

Dolly was about to reply when she heard her name.

"Samson?"

She turned to see Lieutenant Martinez looking from her to Tommy and back.

"Hey, Martinez," she said. "How're you doin'?"

"Not bad. I thought I saw you at the amusement park today, but I wasn't sure. Now I know it was you. I recognize your friend."

"Tommy, this is Carlos Martinez. He also serves on the ship with me."

"Nice to meet you, Carlos."

"Yeah," he said. His dark eyes hardened. "Nice to meet you, too."

"Have you been enjoying liberty?" Dolly asked, although she didn't care. She just wanted him to leave.

"I have. Well, we were just leaving. I'll leave you two to your dinner. See you soon."

"See you."

"He seems like a real asshole," Tommy said.

"He is." She groaned. "He's the last person I would have wanted to see me on a date with a woman. He is the most prejudiced man I've ever met."

"But he's Mexican."

"Doesn't matter. He hates blacks and I'm sure he hates homosexuals."

"Well, again, two women having dinner together doesn't mean they're homosexual."

"You saw the way he looked at you," Dolly said.

"I did. He is filled with hatred."

"Yes, he is."

"Oh well. Seriously, what's the big deal? So he doesn't like that you're gay. No biggie right?"

"I hope not. I can't imagine him using it against me. We're the same rank, so it shouldn't be an issue."

"Good. Now can we order dinner?"

They chatted as they dined, and Dolly felt her apprehension about Martinez slowly dissipate. She didn't know if it was the company, the food, or the wine, but whatever it was, she found herself relaxing and enjoying her meal.

She watched Tommy's lips move as she spoke and fought the strong desire to lean over and kiss her. Later, she told herself. Later, she would have her way with her.

"Are you listening to me?" Tommy said.

Dolly blushed, a deep red that started at her chest and quickly moved upward to cover her face.

"Whoa," Tommy said. "What did I interrupt?"

Dolly just blushed deeper.

"Well, now. I guess if you're not going to listen to me, at least you fantasize about me?"

Dolly finally found her voice.

"I'm sorry. What did you say?"

"I was talking about what we can do tomorrow. But I'd rather hear what you were thinking."

"No. I can't."

"Sure you can. No one's listening to us. Simply lower your voice and say, 'I was thinking about devouring you again.' Simple, really." She laughed.

Dolly's blush deepened further. She didn't know if she'd ever blushed that hard before.

"It was something like that, right?" Tommy pursued the subject. Dolly nodded.

Tommy smiled a devilish grin.

"I knew it," she said.

"Anyway," Dolly said pointedly. "About tomorrow. What do you recommend?"

"I thought we would just wander around town. Maybe hit the aquarium. How does that sound?"

"Sounds wonderful. Our last day together should be special."

"So, tomorrow is your last day of liberty?"

"Yeah. Had I not mentioned that?"

"No. You never told me when it would end."

"I guess I was hoping it never would," Dolly said.

"Me, too."

They sat in silence for a few moments. Dolly felt the weight of her leaving heavy in the air.

"I'm sorry," she said.

"For what?" Tommy said. "It had to happen. I wish you'd have given me a little more notice, but maybe it's actually better this way."

"You think so?"

"Sure. No time to ponder and worry about that day. At least not for me. You've had to fret about it on your own, which isn't really fair, but that was your choice."

"I just kind of wanted to pretend liberty wouldn't end and we'd live like this forever."

"I get that, but reality is setting in. We need to face it."

"I know."

"But not right this minute. There's still tonight and tomorrow."

"And we'll make the most of them, right?" Dolly said.

"You'd better believe it."

"Speaking of making the most of them, shouldn't we be getting back to the motel?"

"I love the way you think," Tommy said. "I really do."

"I can't help it. It's like a constant craving."

"Oh, I'm not complaining. And I get it, believe me. I'm right there with you."

"I'm glad. It wouldn't be fun if this was one sided."

Tommy laughed.

"No. It wouldn't be fun at all."

Tommy paid and they went back to the motel. She sat on the bed and pulled Dolly down next to her. Tommy held Dolly's hand in hers and sat playing with the antique ring she'd bought her.

"I'm not gonna lie. It's not going to be easy to say good-bye to you."

"I know this." Dolly felt a cold fist in the pit of her stomach. She didn't want to think about that horrible moment when they had to say good-bye.

"I just want you to truly understand that. I'm not just saying words. I'm sharing feelings here."

"I know." Dolly couldn't think of anything intelligent to say that wouldn't make the waterworks start.

"And we have to think long-term. Every day of my life isn't like the past few. I'm an activist, Dolly. We'll likely live on a commune and go to protests. You have to be able to do that."

Dolly let Tommy's words sink in. Could she do that? She didn't even know what life on a commune was really like. Was it all free love? Would she have to share Tommy with other women?

"Well, when the war's over, you won't really have anything to protest, will you?"

"There's always something, baby. Land rapers are always at the top of my list."

"And what about life on the commune? Is it all about free love?"

"Free love's everywhere, baby. It's a beautiful thing."

Dolly didn't like the sound of that. She didn't want to share Tommy. She couldn't imagine sharing her with anyone else. She didn't even try to stop the tear that rolled down her cheek.

Tommy wiped it away and tilted her face so she looked into her eyes.

"Baby? What are you thinking? Talk to me."

"I don't want to share you." Dolly started sobbing. The reality of life on a commune hitting home with full force. She felt nauseous from the force of her crying.

"You're not going to share me. Baby, what are you talking about?"

"Free love."

"What about it?"

"I don't want you with other women."

"Oh, baby." Tommy stroked Dolly's hair. "I'm with you. You'll see a lot of free love, but I'm committed to you. I won't be with other women as long as we're together. You don't need to worry about that."

"Oh, thank God." Dolly leaned into Tommy's chest and burrowed against it. She felt Tommy's arms around her. Tommy would be with her and only her. That was a relief. She slowly quit crying and was able to sit up.

"I need to go splash some water on my face," she said. She went into the bathroom and wet her face with cold water. She felt better, but her face was still splotchy and red.

When she walked back to the other room, Tommy was still seated in the same place. She rose and took Dolly in her arms.

"Baby, please. Always talk to me about your fears. That's what I'm here for, okay?"

"Okay. I'm sorry I got so upset. I was just so scared."

"You feel better now?"

"I do."

"Good."

CHAPTER THIRTEEN

Tommy led her back to the bed again and gently pulled her down so she was sitting beside her.

"There's lots about commune life you don't know, but I figure it's probably not all that different from military life in some respects," Tommy said.

"How do you figure?"

"Well, everyone has a role. And if they don't perform their duties, the commune won't run efficiently."

"I suppose that's true. I always just pictured a commune as a big free-for-all."

"Nope. At least not ours. There are people in charge of meals, for example. If they didn't do their jobs, half the commune members would starve."

"Only half?"

"Yep." Tommy laughed. "The other half would make do or not care enough to even notice."

"That's funny."

"But seriously. A commune isn't just a giant orgy. I don't want you thinking it is."

"That's a relief."

"Hey, I know. Maybe tomorrow we could go by the commune. You could meet some people and see the place. It wouldn't be so scary then."

"I don't know," Dolly said.

"What's not to know? I think it's a great idea."

"It's our last day, Tommy. I'd rather just spend it with you."

"You would be spending it with me," Tommy said. "Only we'd be in a place where we can openly hold hands and show affection for each other."

"You know what I mean."

"No, I really don't." Tommy was beginning to get frustrated. She thought if Dolly met some of her friends, it would make the separation easier for her. She didn't understand why Dolly didn't see it.

"I mean, I don't want to share you with other people. I want tomorrow to be like these last few days, where it's just been the two of us."

Tommy understood what Dolly said. And while it would be nice to have another day of just the two of them, wouldn't it be better if Dolly met some of her friends?

"I get that. I just thought it might be good for you to meet some of the people I normally hang out with."

"I'm sorry. Will you be terribly disappointed if we don't?"

Tommy took a deep breath. The truth was, any way she got to spend her last day with Dolly, she'd take.

"No, baby. I just want to enjoy our last day together."

"Good. And if there's enough time at the end of the day, then maybe we do go to the commune, but I don't want that to be a priority, okay?"

"That's cool."

"Good."

Tommy accepted Dolly's suggestion as a possibility they'd actually make it to the commune the next day. This improved her mood substantially. Still, she felt emotionally drained. She grabbed a joint and lit it. After taking a deep puff, she handed it to Dolly. Dolly stared at it and then handed it back to her.

"What's up?" Tommy said.

"I don't want to get all paranoid and stuff again."

"You shouldn't. We're not going anywhere. We're staying in for the rest of the night."

"Okay," Dolly said and took the joint back from Tommy. She took a long drag and gave it back to Tommy.

Tommy took another hit and motioned with the joint to Dolly, who shook her head. Tommy exhaled and put the joint in the ashtray. The nice, mellow feeling settled over Tommy. The angst of the conversation was washed away, replaced by a muted serenity. She sat on the bed next to Dolly again.

"You sure you don't want another hit? It'll make you feel good."

"I'm sure. I feel just fine right now."

"Yeah? You feelin' free and easy?" Tommy said.

"I am."

"Right on. I love the groovy feeling getting stoned gives you."

"Me, too. It washes away all the tension and stress."

"Yeah, it does." She sat silently for a moment. "I wish I could protect you from all tension and stress."

"Thank you. I wish you could, too."

"Someday I'll be able to."

"You really believe that, don't you, Tommy? You really believe that someday lesbians will be treated the same as everybody else."

"Of course I do. I have to. Equality for everyone. I'll die fighting for that."

"Do you think it'll happen in our lifetime?"

"I do. I don't think it's that far off. We just need to educate the bourgeoisie that it's normal and natural, not some sort of aberration."

"And you think people will believe that?" Dolly said.

"Don't you?"

"I guess I do."

"What do you mean, you guess? You don't think there's something wrong with you, do you?"

Dolly sat silently looking at her hands.

"Oh my God. You do think something's wrong. You think you're a freak or something, don't you?"

"I don't know," Dolly said.

"What do you mean you don't know?"

"I don't know," Dolly repeated. "Sometimes I think maybe there is something wrong with me. Maybe if I met the right man, I could settle down and be happy."

"Not me," Tommy said. "I'm a lesbian. I couldn't be happy with a man, nor could I make a man happy. I'm a lesbian and there's nothing wrong with me. I simply love women and not men."

"And you think that's perfectly okay despite what society says?"

"I do. I think society has some pretty fucked up views of a lot of things. Homosexuality being one of them."

"But if you weren't gay, then what?" Dolly asked. "Then would you still think it was okay?"

"I'd like to think so. I believe in equality for everyone, black, white, or gay."

"I wish I was as strong as you, Tommy."

Tommy sat holding her hands while she tried to stomach this latest information.

"So, baby, are you telling me that while you're away, I need to worry about men as well as women stealing you away?"

"I don't think so," Dolly said. "I only want to be with you."

"But if you found a nice man, it would be easier for you and you'd settle down with him, right?"

"That's not fair. That's like me saying if you find a beautiful woman you'll leave me for her."

"That's not even close to the same thing."

"It is. Either we promise to be true to each other or we don't. Man, woman, it doesn't matter. Faithfulness to each other means complete faithfulness."

"I suppose that's true," Tommy said. "But it still bothers me that you think you could be happy with a man if you're planning on spending the rest of your life with me."

"But I didn't meet a man before I met you. You're the one I love and you're the one I want to spend my life with."

"Okay," Tommy said. "I just really want to know you're sure about this."

"I've never been more sure about anything."

Tommy got up and lit the joint again, needing to relax anew. She also poured herself a bourbon and took a glass of wine to Dolly. She sat in the chair at the desk and put her feet on the bed next to Dolly.

"Do you want some of this?" She waved the joint in the air.

"Please."

Tommy handed it to Dolly who took one hit and then another.

"I want to get really stoned."

"You will if you keep doing that."

Dolly took one more long drag before handing it back to Tommy.

"Shit, baby, you're gonna be a mess."

"Oh, well."

Tommy laughed at Dolly. She liked it when Dolly was carefree. She liked it when she herself wasn't stressed about life. Normally she wasn't. She got worked up about issues and fought like hell for what was right, but she wasn't stressed. She didn't believe in it. And staying stoned was one way to stay that way.

Dolly was mumbling something that Tommy couldn't understand.

"What did you say, baby?"

"Huh?"

"I couldn't understand you."

"I didn't say anything."

"Sure you did. You mumbled something."

Dolly started laughing. She laughed so hard she couldn't breathe, and Tommy got worried about her.

"Are you okay?"

Dolly nodded as she rolled over to her side and wrapped her arms around herself, still laughing.

Tommy started laughing, too. She didn't know what was so funny to Dolly, but Dolly was certainly funny enough to make Tommy crack up. Soon there were tears pouring down Tommy's face and her stomach hurt from laughing. She tried to stop, to catch her breath, but then their gazes met and they both started laughing all over again.

Tommy felt like a child, giggling uncontrollably or at least a teenager who couldn't hold her pot. But Dolly was enjoying herself and that was all that mattered. They continued laughing until Tommy deliberately avoided eye contact with Dolly.

"Wow. That was fun."

"Yes, it was. I want always to feel this way, Tommy. Maybe I should take some marijuana on the ship with me."

"That'd be one way to get kicked off and come back to me sooner," Tommy said.

"I know. But it sure would make work more fun."

"Well, I can get you some if you're serious."

"I can't take that chance. If it weren't for that smell, I might just try it, but it reeks."

"Yeah it does. Too bad. I wouldn't mind you taking some with you."

"I'd be laughing at horribly inappropriate times, I'm sure."

"Yeah, that wouldn't be cool."

"Why are you sitting over on the chair? Shouldn't you be on the bed with me?" Dolly said.

"I suppose I should."

Tommy set her drink down and took Dolly's away from her. She sat next to her again and held her face in her hands.

"I love you so much." She kissed Dolly lightly on the lips.

"I love you, too."

Tommy kissed her again, then kissed her cheek and sucked on her earlobe.

"You taste so good." She nuzzled deep against her neck. Dolly leaned back and moaned.

Tommy eased her onto her back and unbuttoned her blouse. She opened it up and played with Dolly's breasts through the confines of her bra. She kissed her cleavage, aroused further by the soft skin. She reflected, yet again, on the perfection of Dolly's body. She loved every curve.

She teased Dolly's nipples so that her bra cups looked like little tents. She knew her nipples were hard and ready for her mouth. Still, she held off unhooking her bra. She ran her hand down her belly and slipped her fingers just inside Dolly's waistband. She felt her muscles ripple in anticipation. Her own nipples hardened at Dolly's response.

Tommy wanted to go slow, to take her time and really make it last. She didn't know if she'd be able to as her desire was growing with each passing second. But she wanted tonight to be special, even if they were both stoned out of their minds.

The room was silent, save for the clock on the nightstand. Every move Tommy made seemed to shatter the silence, only to have it coalesce and return. She finally reached around Dolly, unhooked her bra and freed her breasts. She caught them in her hands and pushed them together. She buried her face between them as she turned her head from side to side to kiss them. They felt wonderful against her cheeks. She wanted to stay like that forever. She pressed Dolly's breasts against her face, molding them to her.

"Does that really feel that good?" Dolly asked.

"You have no idea."

"Good. I want you to feel good."

"Does it feel good to you?" Tommy said.

"It really does."

"Right on."

Tommy stayed like that for a few more minutes before surrendering the breasts and taking a nipple in her mouth. She loved the feel of the large nipple pressed to the roof of her mouth. She sucked as hard as she could and elicited a groan from Dolly. Tommy ran her tongue over the tip of the nipple as she sucked and felt Dolly squirm underneath her. She didn't dare move her mouth, so she dragged her hand down the length of Dolly's body and stopped where her legs met.

"Why are you stopping?" Dolly said.

"Just because."

"Because why?"

"Because I know you want me and I want to drag this out."

"Didn't anyone ever tell you it's not nice to tease?" Dolly said.

"Ah, but sometimes it's fun."

Dolly pulled away from Tommy and quickly stripped off the rest of her clothes. She lay back down and surrendered her body to Tommy.

Tommy went back to suckling Dolly as she ran her fingers over Dolly's hard clit. The feeling of slick warmth made her light headed. She didn't want to get Dolly off too soon, so she rubbed lightly for a few moments before she moved her fingers inside. She stroked Dolly slowly as she plunged her fingers deep.

"Please. I need more," Dolly said.

Tommy smiled to herself. She knew what Dolly needed, but wasn't going to give it to her. Not yet.

She continued to stroke Dolly until Dolly was bucking on the bed, urging Tommy to pump faster, which she did not do. Instead, she pulled out and went back to Dolly's clit.

"You're making me crazy," Dolly said. "I need to come."

"So soon?" Tommy said.

"Yes. Please."

"Okay," Tommy said. She sucked hard on the nipple again while she rubbed Dolly's swollen clit.

Dolly tangled her fingers in Tommy's hair as she moved against her fingers. She was gyrating her hips frantically, seeking release. At last Tommy gave up and moved to just above her clit, the place she knew to be Dolly's favorite and pressed into it.

Dolly screamed as the waves of the orgasm crashed over her. She barely had time to catch her breath when Tommy slid her fingers back inside her and stroked her fast and deep. Dolly arched off the bed, meeting every thrust.

Tommy increased her pace, going faster and faster until she knew Dolly was teetering. She felt her insides quiver around her fingers. She sucked harder on her nipple and moved her fingers as deep as they could go.

Dolly pressed Tommy's head into her chest as she came again and again. And again.

"Oh, my God," Dolly said. "That was amazing."

"Mm." Tommy released her grip on Dolly's nipple. "It really was."

"I can't get over how you make me feel," Dolly said.

"How so? I mean, I know I make you come and all, but what else is there?"

"I don't know if I can explain it. It's so intense. You make me see different colors when I come. It's like I leave my body and watch until it's time to come. Then I float back and then explode into a million little pieces when I climax."

"I don't know, baby. That may just be the pot."

"I don't think so. I think it's something in the way you love me."

"Well, I'd love to take credit, but I really don't think I can."

"I think you should. Please. It's only ever happened with you."

"Well then, thank you. I'm happy to do it. I have to say, you're one of the most fun women I've ever been with."

"Yeah? How so?"

"You're so responsive. Regardless of where I touch, you respond sexually. I think that's great."

"Should I be embarrassed?"

"Only if you're that way with everyone." Tommy laughed. "No. You should definitely not be embarrassed. It's groovy that you're that into me. It makes me feel good."

"Now, will you do me a favor?" Dolly said.

"Anything."

"Take your clothes off so I can ravish your body."

"Gladly."

Tommy stood on unsteady legs. Making love to Dolly always aroused her to the point of shakiness. She managed to get her shirt off.

"What's wrong? Are you okay?" Dolly said.

"I'm fine. Just a little, no, a lot, horny."

"Ah, good."

Dolly lay back on the bed and watched Tommy. Tommy was very aware of Dolly's naked body on display. She tried to step out of her jeans, but almost fell. When she looked over and saw Dolly absently stroking herself, she almost came on the spot.

"That's not fair," Tommy said.

"What's not?" Dolly pretended to be innocent.

"You can't touch yourself like that. Not when I'm having a hard enough time getting my clothes off."

"I thought maybe it would help you do it quicker."

"No. I'm already unsteady 'cause I'm so horny. Seeing you do that is making me crazy. You need to stop right now."

"But it feels so good," Dolly said.

"Oh shit."

Tommy sat on the bed and stripped off her pants, no longer trusting her legs. Once she was naked, she stood again and looked at Dolly whose eyes had closed. She was clearly enjoying herself.

Tommy watched Dolly's fingers work their magic between her legs. She knew exactly what Dolly was feeling, every drop of slickness, every swollen part. She wanted to help her but knew it was too late. Dolly was past help. She was going to get herself off and all Tommy could do was watch.

Dolly stroked her clit and the area around it over and over. Tommy knew she had to be close. She felt moisture trickle down her own leg while watching. There was nothing sexier than watching a woman please herself. She watched as Dolly's breathing became labored. She heard the mewling sounds Dolly always made right before she came. She finally watched Dolly squeeze her eyes shut as she cried out.

"Oh God. Oh dear God. Oh yes."

Tommy laid on the bed with her and pulled her close.

"You know, you're about the sexiest woman I've ever met," Tommy said.

"Really? Because I feel kind of embarrassed now."

"Why?"

"Well, seeing you all discombobulated was really cute and I thought it would be fun to make it even worse for you. So I touched myself. I didn't expect to take it all the way."

"But you did and it was sexy as all hell."

"I'm glad you think so. I'm still a little embarrassed."

"Don't be. All you did was turn me on even more. And wasn't that the goal?"

"I suppose it was. At least to start. At the end the goal was to come." she laughed.

"And you are so sexy when you come," Tommy said.

"So are you," Dolly said.

"Am I?"

"Yes, you are." She rolled on top of Tommy and kissed her. "I love to see you come."

"Good. Because I love to come." Tommy laughed.

"Don't we all?" Dolly said.

Chapter Fourteen

Dolly kissed Tommy hard on the mouth, hoping to convey all her desire and appreciation and love in just one kiss. When the kiss ended, it took Tommy a moment to open her eyes.

"Wow," she said. "That was some kiss."

"I wanted you to know how I feel," Dolly said shyly.

"Baby, I know how you feel."

"I want you to be sure."

"Then show me," Tommy said.

Dolly knew Tommy was past being ready for her. She knew she needed her and Dolly was ready to please her, to take her to new limits of passion. She ran her hand down Tommy's sleek frame, pausing to play with her breasts as she did. She kneaded them and pinched the nipples until they were rock hard and standing at attention. Then she lowered her mouth and pulled one in.

While she suckled, she moved her hand between Tommy's legs. She wanted to tease her some more, but didn't think that would be fair, so she slipped her fingers inside her and caressed her satin walls. She found Tommy's soft spot and paid extra attention to it. Soon, Tommy clamped hard around her fingers as she came for her.

Dolly moved her fingers to Tommy's clit and rubbed lightly.

"I'm too sensitive," Tommy protested.

"What about like this?"

Dolly separated her fingers and stroked her with one finger on either side of Tommy's clit. That seemed to do the trick. She saw Tommy gripping the sheets as she arched off the bed, gurgled something incomprehensible, then fall back onto the bed a limp mess.

While Tommy fought to catch her breath, Dolly snuggled into her arms.

"You know, I'm going to miss all this lovemaking," she said.

"Tell me about it," Tommy said. She pulled Dolly close.

"I think I may even go into withdrawals." Dolly laughed.

"I know I will."

"I love you so much," Dolly said. Somehow it didn't feel like saying it was enough. And she'd just shown her. But it still felt empty. "I don't know. I just don't know how to convey it to you. You know, just how much you mean to me."

"Baby, I know exactly what I mean to you, because it's the same as what you mean to me."

"I hope so. I feel like words are so hollow sometimes. They're only words. And sex is great, but do you really feel the intensity of my emotions?"

"I do feel it. And it's not just during lovemaking. It's when we're together anywhere. Out to dinner or at museums. Not necessarily at the amusement park, but that was different."

"I'm sorry I got so weird today."

"It's okay. For now, society insists we keep our love behind closed doors. And I love what we do behind closed doors."

She kissed the top of Dolly's head.

Dolly rolled over and propped herself up. She looked Tommy in the eye.

"If you were with someone besides me, would you be more open in public?"

"Like hold hands and stuff? Hell no. I have no desire to be lynched. I tell you, I believe it will be a nonissue someday, but that day is not here yet. But would I freak out like you did, just to be seen with another woman? No. I don't think anyone has any idea that we're lovers just because we're at an amusement park together."

"But we've been together for three straight days. Wouldn't you think people would talk?"

"Who's to talk? It's not like we see the same people everywhere we go. The office manager probably pops a boner every time he thinks about the two of us sharing a room, but he's the only one."

"Ew. That's disgusting."

Tommy laughed.

"Yeah, it really is. But my point is, no one knows so no one cares. You just need to relax. And tomorrow we're goin' out again. But no pot for you beforehand. I don't want any paranoia."

"I'm sorry again. I didn't mean to ruin your day."

"You didn't, baby. But I know it wasn't any fun for you to be feeling that way."

"No, it really wasn't," Dolly said. "I just felt like everyone was looking at us and everyone knew."

"And in reality, I'd bet no one even noticed us, much less gave us a second glance."

"I'm sure you're right. I won't get stoned tomorrow so I'll be able to relax and have fun."

"Good. For now, let's go to sleep."

Dolly backed in to Tommy and felt her arms encircle her. She knew it had been the marijuana that had made her so paranoid, because with Tommy's arms around her, she knew she was in the right place.

Dolly woke in the morning and, as usual, Tommy was still sound asleep. Dolly put on slacks and a jacket and went for a walk along the water. She knew Tommy would lecture her when she got back, but what was she supposed to do? Sit around and wait for Tommy to wake up? That would be much too boring.

Dolly walked to the piers and saw the ship she would be leaving on the next day. Grief overcame her at the reality that she would actually be leaving Tommy. She would be back to her regimented life. There would be no more long, slow kisses, no more late night lovemaking. There would be no more Tommy.

The tears came unabated. She was at a loss to stop them. She didn't even try. The cool air helped dry them as she made her way back to the motel and by the time she reached it, she was sure Tommy wouldn't be able to tell she'd been crying.

Tommy was just waking up when she let herself in.

"Where have you been?" Tommy said.

"I went for a walk."

"Yeah? Are you okay? You look like you've been crying."

"Maybe a little."

"What's up? Talk to me."

"Nothing. I just got a little emotional on my walk. That's all."

"What about?" Tommy said.

"Tomorrow."

"Ah, yes. Tomorrow. I refuse to think about that right now. I want only to focus on making today the best damned day it can be. Tomorrow will be here soon enough. Let's not let it get here any sooner."

"I love the way you think."

"And I love you. I hate to see you sad."

"I can't help it. I don't want to say good-bye to you, Tommy."

"Well, you're not saying good-bye to me yet. What do you want to do today?"

"Be with you," Dolly said.

"That's a given. What else?"

"I don't know. You'd mentioned an aquarium. That might be fun. I'd also just like to see the town a little. You know, downtown and all that."

"We could do that. I'll take you on a walking tour."

"That sounds like fun," Dolly said.

"Great. Let's hit the shower."

They took a shower together and Tommy washed Dolly tenderly and lovingly. She didn't do anything sexual, which Dolly was okay with. She just wanted to feel Tommy's hands on her. She simply needed Tommy's touch.

After the shower, they caught a cab downtown and the day started with breakfast at a café across from city hall.

"Do you really have to take cabs everywhere you go?" Dolly couldn't imagine not having her own means of transportation at home.

"I have a van at the commune. I thought about going to get it several times this week, but didn't want to be away from you long enough to do that."

"A van?" Dolly laughed. "I should have known."

"What? I'm a hippie through and through."

"I forget that sometimes. Sometimes, I think you're just Tommy."

"I am Tommy. And Tommy's a hippie and you really shouldn't ever forget that."

"I suppose that's true."

Dolly was silent after that, lost in her thoughts about the differences between herself and Tommy. Again, she questioned what she was doing. How long would they be able to last with her halfway around the world fighting in a war that Tommy was so dead set against? And how long would Tommy be willing to put up with her fighting in that war?

"Baby?" Tommy said. "You ready to order?"

"I'm sorry. No. Give me another minute please?"

She focused on the menu in front of her and was ready when the waitress came back.

"So tell me what I'm seeing," Dolly said as she looked out the window.

"You're seeing city hall and all its administrative buildings. Off to the right, you're seeing Seaview Square. It's like a gathering place for the townsfolk. You know, they have the town Christmas tree there and you can always see people reading or whatnot. Down the road a ways you can make out one of the major shopping centers in town, the Seaview Mall."

"You'd make a great tour guide," Dolly said.

"Thanks. I know my way around the place, that's for sure."

"You do. I can't imagine you spending that much time in this area."

"Sure. We protest in front of city hall all the time. We've sat in at Seaview Square before. And, well, everyone should know where the local mall is."

She laughed, but Dolly didn't laugh with her. Protests. Sit-ins. All so foreign to her.

"What?" Tommy said. "Don't you think everyone should know where the local mall is?"

"Yes," Dolly said. "I was just thinking about the rest of what you said."

"Ah. The protests and sit-ins? Again, baby. I'm a hippie. You know that. You've known that since I first walked up to you on that ship."

"I know. I know. It's just sometimes it's so hard to see you that way. As I said, I only see Tommy when I look at you."

"But that's who Tommy is. Baby, are you having second thoughts?"

"I don't know. I'm having all kinds of worries. I don't know if I'd call them second thoughts, though."

"You need to be perfectly honest with me," Tommy said. "Don't keep any feelings from me. Your feelings affect me in a huge way, so you need to share them with me."

"I'm sorry. I'll do better about that."

"Thanks. So tell me about your worries."

"Just the usual. Me in a war you don't believe in, you here protesting a war I'm sacrificing my life for. It doesn't make sense logically."

"Love knows no logic," Tommy said.

"I suppose that's true."

"You don't sound convinced. Come on. Let's walk."

Tommy paid the bill and they walked over to the square. They found an empty park bench and sat.

"Tell me, Dolly. Are we going to make this work or not?"

"It's not up to just me. It's a two-way street."

"You know I'm dedicated to making it work."

"Are you? Are you really?" Dolly said. "Are you one hundred percent okay that I'm going off to fight in a war you're so dead set against?"

"Dolly, I wouldn't be fine with you fighting in any war. I'll be worried sick about you every moment until you come home to me. The fact that you're fighting in a war I hate so vehemently isn't good, but you signed up for it before you knew me. There's nothing we can do about it at this point."

"I know. And then there's you at the commune. Do you realize that if I did come back here, I'd have no way to get hold of you? What should I do? Stand in the middle of this square and yell your name?"

Tommy laughed.

"I'm serious," Dolly said. "I don't know where you live. I don't know where to send mail. I don't know how to get hold of you in case of an emergency."

"That's part of the joy of living on a commune. We live in our own society, outside of society's norms. I have a PO box if you want to send me letters. I have no phone, though. And I really want to take you to the commune this afternoon so you can see it."

"I suppose that makes sense. Me seeing the commune, I mean. I just know I'm going to wonder about every woman I see."

"What do you mean?"

"I'm going to wonder if you've slept with them."

"Baby, not every woman on the commune likes women. A lot of the free love is between the men and women. Granted, I've been with a few women, but there's no guarantee you're going to see them."

"There's no guarantee I'm not," Dolly said.

"I suppose that's true."

"So I'll wonder."

"I think you're just going to make it harder on yourself if you do."

"Why don't you tell me then?"

"What? You want me to introduce you and say, 'I slept with her'?"

"Not like that. You know what I mean," Dolly said.

"No, I'm not sure I do, but I'll try."

"You don't have to do it when you introduce them."

"Well, I know that. I was being facetious, but I'm not really sure how to do it."

"I don't know. We'll think of something."

"I suppose we will. Besides, like I said, you may not even see anyone I've been with."

They sat quietly for a few minutes while Dolly steeled herself to the idea that she was really going to the commune. It was exciting and terrifying. She wanted to see where Tommy lived and how Tommy lived. But to be surrounded by hippies? These were people she'd been told her whole life were bad people who were dirty freeloaders and violent protesters. The concept that she would interact with them scared her. But Tommy was one. And she was one of the leaders of the group. Maybe these were different kinds of hippies. Dolly hoped.

"Did you want to check out the mall?" Tommy interrupted her thoughts.

"I love to shop," Dolly said.

"Great. Let's go."

Dolly tried to put aside her maudlin thoughts and get herself in a good mood to hit the stores, but it wasn't easy. She was having a hard time enjoying herself. What had Tommy said? Tomorrow would come soon enough? She needed to hold onto that and just have a good time with Tommy now.

They walked into one of the nation's top department stores. It was prom season and all the dresses were on display.

"You'd look great in one of those." Tommy whispered in Dolly's ear.

"Thank you for that vote of confidence, but I don't think so."

"Please try one on. Please? For me?"

Dolly thought Tommy was crazy. Why on earth would she want to see her in one of those dresses? She looked at the dresses and then back at Tommy, where she could see pleading in her eyes.

"Okay. Fine. Which one?"

"This one." Tommy handed her a green shimmering strapless number.

"This one? Are you sure?"

"Baby, I'm positive. Let's find a dressing room."

"You're not coming in with me," Dolly said.

"Why not? I'm just a friend helping you look at a dress."

"Oh my God, Tommy. You're incorrigible."

"Thank you."

Dolly took the dress and they found the dressing rooms. She walked into the spacious area with Tommy right behind her. She kept her focus on Tommy's eyes in the mirror. She stripped out of her clothes while Tommy looked on appreciatively.

"Don't forget your bra," Tommy said.

"I won't."

Dolly took it off, and Tommy was immediately pressed into her back, her hands around her grabbing her breasts.

"Tommy!" Dolly whispered.

"What?" Tommy laughed. She continued to tease Dolly until her nipples were sticking straight up.

"Oh my God. I can barely stand now," Dolly said. "I knew this was a bad idea."

"I could suggest the dress would fit better without underwear."

"No way," Dolly said. "I know better than to fall for that now."

She slipped the dress over her head and Tommy zipped it for her. She had to admire herself in the mirror. She looked damned good.

"Baby, you look amazing." Tommy nuzzled her neck. "I want to buy you this dress and have you wear it to dinner tonight."

Dolly looked down at her cleavage, which threatened to burst out of the dress.

"You don't think it's too much?"

"Too much? I think it's perfect. You're so fucking beautiful, Dolly. I love your body and can't wait to have it again."

"Where on earth would we go to dinner that I could wear this?"

"There's a very formal restaurant here called Top of the Tower. This dress will be perfect."

"What will you wear?"

"I'll find a suit in menswear."

"You sure?"

"Sure I'm sure. On second thought, I won't make it a suit. Just slacks and a jacket. Don't worry. We'll be fine."

"If you insist."

"I do. Now come on, let's get some clothes for me so we can check out."

They found clothes for Tommy and she paid for them and Dolly's dress. She didn't even let Dolly see the price tag. Dolly had gotten used to this over the past few days. She had no idea how much Tommy had spent on her. She was grateful, though and hoped Tommy knew that.

"You do know how much I appreciate everything you've done for me this week," she said.

"Don't even think about it. As you know, I have the means to take care of you and I love doing it."

"I know. But I still want you to know. I don't want you to think I'm taking you for granted."

"I know you're not. You don't need to worry."

"Okay. Thanks."

They wandered in and out of the other shops. Dolly found trinkets in some that she bought and Tommy had her try on clothes in others. They didn't buy any more clothes. Tommy just seemed to like making out in the dressing rooms. Dolly didn't mind herself, if she was honest.

After several hours, Dolly had seen every store in the mall and pleaded fatigue.

"I've done all I can do. I've bought all I need to buy. Let's go relax for a bit."

CHAPTER FIFTEEN

The day was still young when they got back to their motel. Tommy held the door open for Dolly, whose arms were laden with bags.

"Did you have fun?" Tommy asked.

"I had a great time. I told you. I love to shop."

"And shop you did. I don't think I've ever seen someone shop with such voraciousness."

"Now you're embarrassing me."

"Don't be embarrassed. It's charming. Just like everything you do."

"Aw. Thank you."

Dolly loved the little things Tommy said to her that made her feel so special, so loved.

"I think you should try on that strapless dress again," Tommy said.

"If I try that on, it's going to end up a pile on the floor and then I won't be able to wear it tonight. You just be patient."

"But I want you now."

"And you can't have me unless I'm wearing that dress?"

Dolly relaxed on the bed. She leaned back on an elbow and looked at Tommy.

"No," Tommy said. "I want you no matter what you're wearing. I just thought how much fun it would be to peel that dress off you."

"And that's exactly what you will do tonight."

"Mm." Tommy lay down next to Dolly. "And for now?"

"For now, you may take me as I am."

"Sounds good to me. Let's get out of these clothes."

Dolly stood and stripped. She loved taking her clothes off in front of Tommy. She always seemed so appreciative.

"You're so fuckin' foxy," Tommy said.

"Thank you." Dolly blushed.

Tommy stood before her, her lithe body looking inviting. Dolly stepped into her arms. At first they simply held each other, Dolly reveling in the strength of Tommy's arms. Eventually, Tommy tilted Dolly's face up to hers and kissed her. She moved her tongue slowly around Dolly's mouth. The kiss made Dolly's toes curl.

"Let's lie down," Dolly said.

They lay down together and limbs entwined with limbs, tongues with tongues as they sought to hold on to the passion that raged between them. Dolly was dizzy with need as they moved together on the bed. She cried out loud when Tommy finally granted her release.

"That was amazing, Tommy."

"That really was special, wasn't it?"

Dolly ran her hand between Tommy's legs.

"I'm fine, baby," Tommy said.

"How is that possible?"

"I came when you did."

"You did?" Dolly asked.

"It was so intense. And when you came, I did, too. That's never happened to me before."

"Wow. That's really cool."

"I thought so."

They lay together on the bed. Dolly felt like a pile of noodles. She didn't think her bones would ever come back.

"We should shower," Tommy said.

"Why?"

"I don't want to get to the commune too late."

Dolly's stomach cramped at the thought. She was terrified of seeing the commune. And even though Tommy said it wasn't a giant orgy, she knew she'd look at every woman and wonder if they'd been together. There was a cold fist clamping her insides. She didn't want to go.

On the other hand, it was only fair to see where Tommy lived, how Tommy lived. She had no idea what a commune was like. None whatsoever. She'd never been to one and had never paid much attention if she ever heard anyone talk about them, which was infrequently. She might have heard some of her shipmates bad-mouthing communes, but she'd never listened too closely.

And it was important to Tommy. That was the bottom line. It was important to Tommy so it was important to her.

"Okay," she finally said. "Let's go get in the shower."

In the shower, their lovemaking continued, with Tommy slowly caressing Dolly until she floated through another orgasm.

"You're so amazing at that," Dolly said.

"You're easy to love."

"Lucky me."

"Lucky us."

Dolly laughed and quickly finished her shower. They got dressed and Tommy held her arms straight out and rested her hands on Dolly's shoulders.

"Baby, I know this isn't easy for you," she said. "But I want you to know how much I appreciate this. I think it's important."

"I know it's important, Tommy. I really do. But you're right. It's hard for me."

"But it's where I live. Aren't you even mildly curious about that? I know I'd love to see where you call home. Especially in Atlanta. It would be wonderful to see where little Dolly grew up. But even now. I'd like to see your place. How is it decorated? You know, things like that."

"Okay, okay. I get it. And yes. I admit, I'm more than mildly curious. It's not your place I'm worried about. It's the people. And you know that."

"I promise to tell you if we run into someone I've slept with, okay?"

"Okay. That's fair."

"All right, then. Let's go."

"How will we get there?" Dolly asked.

"We'll walk. It's not far."

"Okay."

They started out across the motel parking lot, then cut through some trees. Dolly tried to memorize the path they were taking, but soon gave up and simply followed Tommy. Eventually, they came to a large clearing filled with tents.

"Welcome to my home," Tommy said.

Dolly took it all in. She thought it would be incredibly uncomfortable to live in a tent full time. She stood on the edge of the clearing and watched the people milling about. They seemed perfectly happy, though. And Tommy certainly enjoyed it. Although, she admitted she went to town on occasion to get a break from it all.

"Come on," Tommy said. "I'll show you my place."

"Okay." Dolly braced herself, unsure of what was to come.

Tommy took her hand and led her through the maze of tents until they came to a spacious red one.

"This is home." Tommy held the flap open and Dolly walked in.

The tent was somewhat neat, though not nearly as spic-and-span as Dolly's quarters on the ship. Her sleeping bag was on a cot against the far wall. On the near wall was a long table with propane apparatuses on it—a coffee maker, a grill, and the like.

There was a trunk against another wall that was open with clothes spewing forth.

"Looks like you left here in a hurry," Dolly said. She motioned to the trunk.

"We were going out. I just rummaged through until I found what I wanted to wear. I figured I'd clean up the next morning. Little did I know I wouldn't be home for three or four days."

"That makes sense. I like your little world," Dolly said.

"Thanks. It's not much, but it's home. And it's how I like to live."

"You're lucky you get to live how you want," Dolly said.

"Hey, baby, you're the one who chose to go into the navy."

"I know. I shouldn't complain."

Tommy put her arm around Dolly and pulled her close.

"It's okay. You can always complain around me." Then she said, "So, have you ever made love in a tent?"

"Oh my God, Tommy. Don't you feel like you're making love in front of the whole commune when you do that?"

"Not necessarily."

"I would."

"I'd close and tie off the door so no one could interrupt us." She kissed Dolly.

"Seriously. Then they'd know for sure what we were doing."

"So? It's natural, baby. It's all about love. No one would think a thing."

"I can't, Tommy. I'm sorry."

"I'm sorry, too. You look so cute here among my things. I really want you again, but I'll wait. Come on. Let me show you around the commune."

Dolly felt the familiar discomfort return.

"We don't have to look around," she said. "I've seen your home. That's the important thing."

"Baby, these people are my friends. My family. It's important to me that you meet them. Now, come on."

She took Dolly's hand and led her out of the tent. She crossed the commune with her until they came to the dining area.

"I suppose this is what you'd call a mess hall," Tommy said. She took Dolly into the main area and then behind it to show her the kitchen.

"Hey, Tommy. Where've you been?" a woman asked.

"Trinity, this is my girlfriend, Dolly. Dolly, Trinity."

"Nice to meet you," Trinity said. "So someone finally snared Tommy, huh?"

Dolly shook hands with Trinity, but raised her eyebrow at Tommy. She'd finally snared her, huh? She wondered anew just how many women Tommy had been with. Clearly she had a bit of a reputation. Dolly felt a twinge of unease. Had Trinity been with Tommy?

"Very funny," Tommy laughed. "It's not so hard to believe."

"Well, it's nice to meet you anyway, Dolly," Trinity said and turned back to her work.

Tommy took Dolly outside again.

"Hey, baby," she said in a low voice. "If anyone asks what you do, tell them you're a nurse, okay? Don't mention the navy or anything like that."

"Don't worry. I won't. So, have you slept with her?"

"Who?" Tommy looked around.

"Trinity."

"No."

"Okay."

"You really are going to worry about every woman you meet, aren't you?" Tommy said.

"I said I would."

"Fair enough. But you don't have to."

"I will, though, just the same."

Tommy led Dolly throughout the commune and they ran into several people. Most of them were men with long hair and beards and a serious lack of deodorant. When they were out of earshot, Dolly finally said something to Tommy.

"How can you stand the smell of these guys?"

"Not everyone cleans up regularly. We don't judge them."

"You may not judge them, but how can you stand to be around them?"

"I suppose we get used to the smell," Tommy said.

"I can't imagine."

Tommy laughed and they continued their tour. The back of the commune opened up on a beautiful creek.

"I spend a lot of time fishing here," Tommy said.

"It's beautiful. I wish we'd have brought fishing poles. I'd love to try my hand at it."

"We can go back and get them."

"No. We don't want to be late for this fancy dinner you have planned for us."

"True," Tommy said.

They cut back through the trees until they arrived at the commune again.

"So what do you think of my home?" Tommy said.

Dolly was silent as she thought of just how to answer the question. What did she think about Tommy's home? She actually found it somewhat barbaric. The lack of basic sanitation was too much for her. She could never live on a commune. That was for sure.

"I think it's an interesting way to live. I think I'd have to spend a few days here in order to really get a feel for it," she said.

"I suppose that's true. You can't really get the whole experience just wandering around it one afternoon."

"No."

"Okay, well, let's get home so we can get ready for dinner."

"Home?" Dolly laughed.

"Back to the motel. You knew what I meant."

"I did. Okay, let's go."

They held hands until they came to the border of the commune. Then Dolly gently pulled hers away from Tommy and they walked the rest of the way in silence.

"So how fancy is this place we're going tonight?" Dolly said.

"Fancy enough for you to wear that dress and fit right in."

Dolly thought for a moment, before deciding to apply a little makeup to dress herself up more. She opted for mascara to bring out her eyes, a slight brushing of blush, and some pink lipstick. She looked in the mirror and was satisfied, but when she turned to face Tommy, she knew she'd made the right decision.

Tommy's face was lit up.

"Oh, my God. You're gorgeous," Tommy said.

"Thank you." Dolly blushed.

"No. I mean it. You are unbelievably gorgeous."

Dolly felt the blush deepen. She didn't know what to say. She stood there looking at her feet.

Tommy lifted Dolly's face so she could see her. She lowered her mouth to kiss her, and Dolly let herself forget everything in the world except that kiss. There was no commune, no tomorrow, no nothing but the feel of Tommy's mouth on hers.

The kiss finally ended, and they were both breathing heavily.

"Now I need to reapply my lipstick," Dolly said.

"I'd say I'm sorry, but I'd be lying."

"You're so funny. Okay. Let's go, Dapper Dan."

"Dapper Dan, huh? So, you like the suit?"

"I do. You look very handsome, if that's okay to say."

"Sure. I don't mind being considered a handsome woman."

"Good. Because I think you're the handsomest woman on earth."

"Handsomest? Is that a word?"

"It is now."

"Fine," Tommy laughed. "Let's hit the road."

They took a cab downtown to a nondescript looking building. They got out and went inside. There was a line by a stand over by the elevators.

"I'll go put our name in."

Dolly looked around as she waited. Nothing, not a thing, about the place seemed special. Though, she did note that everyone was dressed as formally as she and Tommy. It was a strange sensation to have people all dressed up in a lobby of what could be any business building downtown.

Tommy was back.

"He said we have about a twenty-minute wait. He did say there are seats at the bar, if you want to wait there."

Dolly looked around. She saw no bar. She saw no restaurant. She also saw no place to sit where they were, so she figured an imaginary bar would be better than where they were.

"Let's go to the bar," she said.

"Great," Tommy said. She led them through the few couples waiting and pushed the up button on the elevator.

"Ah, this makes more sense."

"What does?"

"Getting on the elevator. I was beginning to think you all were delusional there."

"Very funny." Tommy laughed.

The elevator arrived and Tommy pushed the top floor. The elevator sped past the intermediate floors until it came to a gentle stop. The doors opened and Dolly was transported into a wonderful new world. It was a dark room, done in navies and blacks. The lights were muted, the music low. But the view!

"What an amazing view," Dolly said. "I can see forever out the windows."

The windows went all around the floor, so the view of the city was available no matter where you looked.

"Isn't it beautiful?"

"It really is," Dolly said.

They pushed through the crowd at the bar and Tommy ordered their usual drinks for them. They sat in some soft chairs at a low table and sipped them.

"I love this place," Dolly said.

"Good. I knew you would."

Dolly looked out the windows in front of them and could see the docks. She saw what she assumed was her ship waiting for her to depart on the next day. The thought made her sad, very sad. She felt the tears in her eyes and fought to keep them from spilling over. The last thing she wanted was mascara running down her cheeks.

"Are you okay?" Tommy said.

"Yes." Dolly took a napkin and dabbed at her eyes.

"Why are you sad?"

"Just thinking about tomorrow."

"No, no. Please don't. Not now. We'll worry about that tomorrow. Let's just enjoy the night."

"I do so wish I could be more like you," Dolly said.

"No," Tommy said. "You need to be you. Because that's who I love."

"Now you're going to make me cry again."

"No more tears."

"Okay. I'll try."

They were called to their table, which was on the other side of the restaurant. It afforded them a completely different view of the city, though just as stunning. Lights twinkled off in the distance. Dolly was captivated.

"I can't get over the views from this place." She sipped her second glass of wine.

"I knew you'd love it."

"I really do."

The waiter took their order and they ordered more drinks, too. Dolly was getting a good buzz going.

"I suppose I'd better slow down on these drinks," she said.

"Why? You deserve to go out with a bang."

"I can't show up to the ship hung over."

"Why not?"

"Seriously, Tommy. That wouldn't go over very well with the higher-ups."

"You know how I feel about the higher ups."

"Unfortunately, they run my life. And that life starts again tomorrow, whether I like it or not."

"I can't imagine living my life taking orders from someone else," Tommy said.

"It's actually a lot of someone elses, not just one."

"That's even worse."

"Tommy, let's not talk about that. Not now."

Dolly found herself frustrated by Tommy's attitude. She should respect what Dolly did, even if she didn't agree with it. But she knew that wasn't going to happen. And she asked herself if she respected Tommy's calling. Not really. What was she thinking? How could this relationship last?

"Whatcha thinkin'?" Tommy asked.

"Nothing," she said. "Just pondering reality."

"Ah yes. Reality. I thought we agreed not to worry about that tonight."

"We did. But sometimes I think."

"You think too much, baby. Relax and enjoy the evening."

"I'm trying."

But Dolly couldn't shake her unease. The very basis of a relationship was trust. Did she trust Tommy? Somewhat. Not really. Not on the commune with other women and free love. The other basis was respect. That was something neither of them had. She was beginning to wonder if they were making a grave mistake. Maybe they shouldn't try to make it last.

She sipped her next glass of wine and made herself stop her silly way of thinking.

"Do you ever get out of town? You know, travel anywhere?" she said.

"Random," Tommy said. "But yes, I do. Depends where I need to protest. If there's a big development that's cutting down lots of trees, I'll be there."

"Even if it's your dad's company?"

"Especially if it's Dad's company. He's made enough money. He doesn't need to kill any more trees."

"Wow. I can't imagine feeling that way."

"Well, your father probably hasn't been able to set up a never ending trust fund for you, has he? How many servants do your folks have? How many houses and estates?"

"I guess I see your point. We only have the one house I grew up in and we have no servants. And God knows I don't have a trust fund."

"Yep. He's got more money than God. He doesn't need to keep raping the land."

Their dinner arrived and they chatted while they ate.

"I bet your folks are really down to earth," Tommy said.

"They are."

"They did a really good job raising you."

"Thank you. I think your folks did a great job raising you, too. I really like you."

"I really like you, too." Tommy laughed. She signaled for the waiter and ordered two more drinks.

"How can you not be sloshed?" Dolly said.

"I can hold my booze okay. How are you doing?"

"I'm getting drunk."

Tommy laughed again.

"No harm in that, like I said. I think you should relax and be totally at ease tonight."

"Well, I don't want to be too drunk for later, if you know what I mean."

"Oh, you won't be."

CHAPTER SIXTEEN

They finished their dinner and Tommy hailed a cab for them. The night was warm, made warmer by the large amount of bourbon she'd drank. She looked over at Dolly, whose breasts were barely held in by the fabric of the dress, and her hormones surged. She couldn't wait to get back to the motel and have her way with her. She noted that Dolly was rather inebriated and wondered what drunk lovemaking with her would be like. Would it be sloppy? Frenzied? She had no way of knowing. She smiled to herself. The unknown was often quite enjoyable.

They got back to the motel and Dolly smiled at Tommy.

"So, how long do I have to stay in this dress?" she said.

"Not long," Tommy said. "Not long at all."

She ran her hands up and down Dolly's arms.

"You're so soft, so smooth," she said.

"Thank you."

She brought her hands up to gently stroke her cleavage.

"So very soft."

Tommy kissed her then, tenderly, her tongue lightly running along Dolly's bottom lip. Dolly would have none of that, though. She put her hands behind Tommy's head and pressed her into her. She plunged her tongue into Tommy's mouth.

Tommy went along with it, her own passion flaring. If Dolly wanted it fast and furious, then that's how Dolly would get it. She unzipped Dolly's dress and lifted it over her head. She stared in amazement at Dolly's breasts.

She hastily stripped off her own shirt and undershirt and stood, feeling Dolly's breasts against hers. They stood nipple to nipple and the connection was almost too much for Tommy to bear. Dolly was kissing her frantically again and digging her fingernails into Tommy's back.

Tommy wondered if the sex might be rough that night. She'd not had rough sex with Dolly yet, but she'd not had drunk sex with her either. Maybe that's just how Dolly got when she got drunk.

Tommy stepped out of the rest of her clothes while Dolly did the same. They lay on the bed and Dolly straddled Tommy. She ground into her while she played with her breasts. Tommy thought she might short circuit from her arousal. Seeing Dolly teasing her own breasts was making her crazy. She was kneading them and twisting her nipples. She finally bent over and sucked a nipple into her mouth.

"Oh dear God. That's so fucking sexy," Tommy said. She moved under Dolly and felt her pelvis coated with Dolly's juices.

"You like that, huh?" Dolly said.

"Shit yeah. You're sexy as hell."

Dolly leaned forward so her breasts dangled over Tommy's face.

"You want these?" she said.

The sight of them dangling there was too much for her to take. Tommy grabbed one with both hands and pulled it to her. She sucked greedily, as if her life depended on it. She moved her tongue over it as she sucked it further into her mouth. She released the one and repeated her actions with Dolly's other breast. She was soaking wet and needed more.

She pulled Dolly to her and kissed her passionately. She slipped her tongue into Dolly's open mouth and tangled it around her tongue. The action only fueled her need.

Dolly rolled off Tommy, allowing Tommy to move her hand between Dolly's legs where she found her wet and ready for her.

She slid her fingers inside Dolly, who spread her legs wider to allow her to go deeper.

"Fuck me, Tommy. Fuck me good."

Dolly's attitude only made Tommy crazier. She loved the licentious way Dolly was behaving. She loved the reckless abandon she was allowing herself to act with. This was a side of her she'd never seen. A side she'd like to see more of.

"Give it to me," Dolly said. "I want more."

Tommy slipped another finger inside and Dolly moaned. Tommy was loving the feel of Dolly's juices flowing down her forearm. She added yet another finger to see if Dolly could take it and she did.

"Oh God, yes. That feels amazing," Dolly said.

Tommy was frenzied by that point. Fucking Dolly wasn't enough. She needed to do more. She longed to taste the copious amounts of fluid that were pouring forth from her. She slid down her body and ran her tongue over her clit. Her flavor was heady, intoxicating. She continued to move her fingers in and out while she licked and sucked her swollen clit until Dolly tangled her fingers in her hair. She arched into her, was still, then relaxed back onto the bed, spent.

"You were amazing," Tommy said. "I like it when you're reckless."

"I was horny as hell."

"I still am."

"But not for long," Dolly said as she slipped her fingers inside Tommy.

"Oh yeah, that's it," Tommy moaned as she moved against Dolly. "That feels so fucking good."

"You like that, huh? You want more?"

"Please. Give it to me, baby."

"You got it." She plunged her fingers deeper and faster until Tommy was writhing on the bed under her. She arched her hips and gyrated, making sure Dolly hit every spot inside her. Finally, she felt the pressure build in her center. It grew to an almost painful point and then it blew up, the pressure released and a warm current spread throughout her body.

She felt completely satiated, but wasn't sure how Dolly was doing. She'd been so aroused. She ran her hand down her body again until she was inside her.

"Oh, more? Thank you," Dolly said.

"My pleasure." Tommy stroked her until she cried out again and again as she rode one orgasm after another.

When Tommy was sure Dolly had had enough, she climbed up next to her on the bed and pulled her into a loving embrace. The unwanted thought crept in that in a few short hours Dolly would be gone. She couldn't stand the thought of it, but was confident that their love was strong enough to withstand the distance to come and the differences they had. She almost said something to Dolly, but heard her soft sleeping sounds and didn't want to disturb her.

Tommy woke up the next morning to find Dolly in her white nurse's uniform. She was sitting on the desk chair looking at Tommy.

"How long have you been up?" Tommy said.

"A couple of hours."

"How are you feeling?"

"Hung over as hell."

Tommy laughed.

"It's really not funny," Dolly said.

"I'll bet you dollars to doughnuts you won't be the only one."

"That may be true. I still don't like feeling this way."

"But did you have fun?" Tommy said.

"I did."

"Good. That's all that matters."

"I suppose you're right. And it was fun."

"Come sit on the bed with me," Tommy said.

"No, I don't think that's a good idea."

"Hey, baby. I see you're already dressed, I'm not going to try to molest you. I just want you to come sit with me."

"I think we need to talk," Dolly said.

Tommy didn't like the sound of that. Her stomach clenched in a fist of fear. Sure, she knew they needed to talk about the logistics of their relationship, but there was something in Dolly's tone that scared her to death.

"You mean about how we're going to keep this going while you're gone?" Tommy said hopefully.

"I mean in general."

"Baby, I don't like your tone. You're scaring me."

"I've been thinking," Dolly began.

"Oh shit. No, you haven't. Don't say anything more. I don't want to hear it. We'll be fine, baby. I promise."

"It's asking a lot for us to make it through the rest of my time. Sure, I'm only on this tour for six months, but who knows where my next tour will take me? And who knows when we'll see each other again?"

"So you're telling me these past few days have been a lie? You've had no intention of making a relationship with me?" She couldn't believe her ears. Dolly had seemed as committed as she had been. She'd been loving, attentive, caring. And now she was basically telling her to go to hell without her.

"No, I'm not saying that. I do love you, Tommy. I'll always love you. I just don't think we're right for each other."

"And just when did you decide this?" Tommy said.

"I don't know."

"You don't know? When was it, Dolly? Yesterday? The day before? This morning? When did you realize we weren't going to make it?"

"Last night."

"Before or after we made love?"

Dolly looked at her feet. She didn't answer.

"At dinner? Is that when? At our last meal together?"

"That's when I started having my doubts," Dolly said.

"And you said nothing," Tommy said. "And you let me make love to you last night."

Tommy was disgusted. She felt used and dirty.

"I still love you, Tommy. I don't think you're hearing me."

"If you loved me, you wouldn't dump me."

"Tommy, please listen to me. I do love you. But I think we're too different to make this work."

"What would you need from me?" Tommy said. "How would I need to change to make it work?"

"Would you really be willing to change?" Dolly said.

Tommy stared at her. No, she wouldn't. She wouldn't change for anyone. Either Dolly loved who she was or she didn't.

"No. I like who I am. I won't apologize for it."

"And you don't need to. But eventually, my serving in the war would get too much for you or your protesting it would get too much for me."

"You're making assumptions. We don't know either of those things. Or maybe you do. Maybe my protesting has been an issue with you from the beginning and you just wanted a liberty fuck."

"It wasn't like that and you know it," Dolly said.

"I'm not sure I know anything. I certainly don't know you."

"Tommy, please, you're not making this easy."

"And you thought it would be? You thought you could tell me to fuck off and I'd be okay with it? I'd just go back to my commune and forget about you, us, the past few days, the future I thought we had?"

"I don't know," Dolly had tears in her eyes.

"Oh no. Don't you dare. Don't you dare cry or act like this isn't all your fault. I won't feel bad for you. This is all on you. It came out of left field and blindsided me. I should be the one crying. You're the one breaking my heart."

"But you're making it sound like I don't love you. And I do. I just don't think we'll be able to make it work." The tears were trickling down her cheek. Tommy hardened herself against them.

"If you loved me you'd at least be willing to try. But you're not. That's what I don't understand."

"I just don't think it would work."

"So you've said," Tommy said. She was angry and frustrated and at a loss of what to do. "Maybe you should leave."

"I don't want to leave like this. I want us to at least be civil. I was hoping we could be friends."

"I don't make a habit of becoming friends with people who cut me to the quick."

"Tommy, please. Think about it. I'm off with the baby killers you hate. Eventually, you'd give up on me."

"You don't know me, do you?" Tommy said. "You didn't get to know me at all over your liberty. I love you. I don't like that you're in the navy, but I'm past that. I don't believe in the baby killing that's going on. You know that. But I don't think you do, either. You're simply following orders. I believe that. So I'm okay with what you're doing, to a degree."

"To a degree, yes," said Dolly. "But not completely. We need to respect what each other does in order to have a relationship and let's be honest. We don't."

"Because you don't respect me as an activist?" Tommy said.

Dolly didn't respond.

"You really don't," Tommy said. "You don't respect what it is I believe so wholeheartedly in. And you just played along with me over the past few days, acting like it was no big deal. How could you?"

"I guess it's that I don't understand. I don't understand how you can live in a tent all your life and then protest when it's time, then go back to your tent. It makes no sense to me. To not have more to do with your life than spew hatred."

"Spew hatred? Look, we are in a war that we don't belong in. Kids are dying in this war. The people have the right to be heard. I'm part of the people. I make sure our voices are heard."

"See what I mean? We're two different people. You speak out against the war and I help people injured in the war. We're at two different ends of the spectrum."

"And you've known that since I approached you on the dock when you first stepped off that ship," Tommy said. "Yet you proclaimed your love for me. You made me feel happy, special, loved. Now I feel dirty and used."

Tommy felt grimy all over. She felt like she'd bathed in grease. She climbed out of bed and headed to the bathroom. She took a long shower, trying to wash off the dirty feeling she had, but it didn't work. She toweled off and walked back to the bedroom to see Dolly still seated at the desk.

"You're still here." She'd hoped Dolly would leave while she showered.

"Yes, I am. I can't leave until we've resolved this. I can't go while you hate me."

"This isn't going to get resolved," Tommy said. "There's nothing to resolve. You called it off. That's all there is to it."

"But I don't want you to hate me," Dolly said.

"Maybe after some time I won't. But for now, I can't help it."

"Fair enough. I've written down my address for you. You know, in case you ever decide to write."

"Don't count on it."

"I won't."

Dolly stood. Tommy couldn't believe the moment was at hand. She'd dreaded it each day they'd had together. And now it was here and she was happy to see Dolly go after what she'd done to her heart. Still, a part of her mourned the loss of the relationship they'd had.

"I guess I'd better go," Dolly said.

"Don't let the door hit you."

"This isn't how I wanted things to end."

"I didn't want things to end at all, so I guess we're somewhat even," Tommy said.

Dolly stepped over to Tommy and wrapped her arms around her. Tommy stood rigid with her arms at her sides. Dolly backed away slowly.

"Okay. I see," she said.

Tommy said nothing. Dolly picked up her suitcase and walked to the door.

"I'm going to miss you, Tommy."

"Don't bother. You'll be busy with your war and I'll be busy trying to end it."

"I wish it didn't have to be like this."

"It was your choice," Tommy said.

"I didn't mean for it to end like this. Oh well. There's nothing we can do now. I need to report for duty. Take care, Tommy."

"Good-bye."

Tommy closed the door behind Dolly but pulled the curtain back so she could watch her walk to the dock. It hurt like hell to watch the only woman she'd ever loved walk out of her life.

She moved away from the window and sat on the edge of the bed. She buried her face in her hands and cried.

CHAPTER SEVENTEEN

Tommy looked around the room she'd shared with Dolly those few days. All she wanted to do was crawl back into bed and go to sleep. Then maybe she'd wake up and it would have all been a nightmare and Dolly would still love her and they could live happily ever after.

But she knew that wasn't going to happen. Still, sleep sounded so good. It was one of her favorite escape mechanisms. She had to check out, though, so sleep wasn't an option. Instead, she fired up a doobie and took a few hits. There, that helped. She was feeling mellow and relaxed and able to move on with her day, if not her life.

She grabbed a duffle bag they had picked up on one of their shopping sprees and shoved all her clothes in it. Not that she would need these clothes on the commune, she reasoned she might need them at some point in the future so she opted to keep them. With a full duffle bag, she walked to the office, paid their bill, and started her trip back to the commune.

She walked across the parking lot, unable to believe it had just been the day before that she'd taken this trip with Dolly. She'd been so excited to show her where she lived and introduce her to her friends. She'd had no idea Dolly had been play acting the whole time.

Tommy cut through the underbrush and came out on the open area that was home. Her heart felt lighter than it had all morning. She was home. Home. A place where people loved her for who she was. A place where no one acted one way when they felt another. Home. A place where Dolly could no longer hurt her.

She made her way through the tents to hers and set her duffle bag down. She lay down on her cot and laced her fingers behind her head. She stared at the ceiling and replayed every moment of the past few days. She wondered what she'd missed. Had there been any signs that Dolly hadn't really been in love with her? Sure, Dolly said she still was, but Tommy was certain that was just her way of feeling better about herself. She didn't think Dolly had ever loved her.

Tommy would have been fine simply having a fling with Dolly. She would have entered that enthusiastically. She loved no-strings-attached sex. But Dolly had been different. Or so she'd thought.

She was educated, intelligent, and soft-spoken. And her eyes. Her eyes had been so animated. One could see everything she was thinking and feeling in those eyes. Tommy tried to shake off the depression she was feeling, but couldn't. She lay like that for what seemed like hours until sleep finally overtook her.

She woke up unsure of where she was, but the events of the day came back and hit her full force. She sat on the edge of her cot and rubbed her eyes. She checked her watch. Two o'clock. After lunch and before dinner. And she was hungry. She reached for one of the joints she'd taken to town that fateful night and found them gone. She rolled another and took several hits. This made her feel better, though she was still hungry. She headed to the dining hall to see if she could find something to munch on.

She found Trinity relaxing with a book.

"Hey, Trinity," she said. "Are there any leftovers in the fridge?"

"Sure. Help yourself. Where's your girlfriend today?"

"Truth?"

"Truth," Trinity said.

"She dumped me this morning."

"Oh, I'm sorry to hear that. She seemed like a nice woman."

"Yeah. She really did," Tommy said.

She helped herself to leftovers and had just finished when a man came running in.

"The ship's set to leave. Everyone to the dock."

In her stoned state of mind, it took Tommy a minute to realize they needed to protest a navy ship. It took her another minute to realize Dolly would be on it. She got up and hurried with the rest of the gang to the dock. Some held signs. Some chanted. But Tommy couldn't help herself. She yelled at the top of her lungs, hoping somehow Dolly would hear her above the others.

"Fuck you, baby killers!" she said. Someone picked up on it. Then another and soon the whole group was chanting it at the ship. Still, Tommy tried to yell the loudest. She wanted her voice screaming at her to be the last thing Dolly heard before she left town.

After the ship had pulled out of dock, Tommy walked with the rest of her group back to the commune. Most people were jumping around or dancing, high after the protest. Tommy tried to feel their happiness. Or anything. But she felt nothing. Only numbness. She tried to tell herself she felt vengeance at cussing at Dolly for what she'd done to her, but she didn't. Dolly was gone. They were through and Dolly was really gone. Her heart was broken.

It was almost dinner time by the time they got back to the commune. Needing to keep herself busy, Tommy went to the dining hall to help with dinner preparations. She was given some tasks to do that kept her hands occupied, but not her mind. Still, it beat sitting in her tent wallowing in her sorrows.

"Hey, Tommy, you okay?" Jimmy, a man about her age with long blond hair stopped at her station.

"I'm okay, why?"

"You're not yourself. You're awfully quiet."

"Rough day," Tommy said.

"Sorry to hear that, man. Hey, I haven't seen you around in a while. Where you been?"

"I met up with a townie and thought we were in love. Was with her for a few days."

"Yeah, but it didn't work out?"

"No. She let me know that this morning."

"Bummer. I'm sorry."

"Yeah. I didn't see it coming, you know?"

"That's the worst," Jimmy said. "When it's all one-sided."

"Yep." Tommy really didn't want to talk about it anymore. She was afraid she'd start crying again and she couldn't bear the thought of the people on the commune seeing her cry. To them, she was a fierce, strong leader. Not a wimp.

"Well, if you need to talk about it or anything, my tent's always open."

"Thanks, man."

He walked off and she took a deep breath. She finished her tasks and asked Trinity if there was anything else she could do. She was told no so she went back to her tent. Feeling more alone than she'd ever felt in her life, she smoked some more pot and decided to wander around the commune and see what everybody was up to.

People were gathered in circles, playing cards or dominoes or backgammon. Or just sitting with friends enjoying the quiet evening. She searched deep inside herself, hoping to find the familiar serenity that she felt when she was home, but it wasn't there. She felt restless and edgy.

The bell finally rang signaling that dinner was ready. Tommy walked to the dining hall with some friends, but felt separate from them. She hated feeling like she didn't fit in. She told herself she was just out of sorts because her heart was broken, but deep down she wondered if she'd ever feel like she fit in again.

Dinner was good, but Tommy just sat there lost in her own thoughts while conversations went on around her.

"Hey, Tommy." Jimmy had walked up and she hadn't even noticed.

"Yeah?"

"You're takin' that tuning out too seriously." He laughed. So did she, though hers was hollow. "I mean it, man. Come on. Get with us. A group of us are going to go make some music. Come watch. It'll do you good."

Tommy walked with Jimmy to the circle area where the drums had already started. Jimmy fired up a joint and took a hit then passed it to Tommy. She took a deep drag and handed it back.

"Take another hit," he said. "I need to go get my guitar."

Tommy did as instructed while she watched him walk off in the direction of his tent. The drums made the ground shake slightly, and Tommy struggled to stay upright. She found that moving from foot to foot helped her keep her balance.

Jimmy was back with his guitar and Beldon was blowing into his harmonica. Tiffany was playing her tambourine. The music was soulful, and Tommy was soon lost in the melody. They simply improvised for a while as a crowd gathered, then they began to play songs everyone could sing along with.

They played Jimi Hendrix and Janis Joplin. They played the Grateful Dead and the Doors. Tommy allowed herself to think of happier times, like when she had gone to the Monterey Pop Music Festival with a group from the commune a couple of years before. They'd had more fun there. She belonged with these people, she realized. Fuck Dolly if she didn't want her. These people did and she had them and always would.

Tommy was tired. It had been a long and difficult day. She cut out of the circle and walked back to her tent where she fell into a restless sleep. She had nightmare after nightmare about bombs dropping on the commune and babies covered in blood. She woke up at eight the next morning and opted to stay awake, not wanting any more bad dreams.

She dragged herself out of bed and pulled on some clothes, then made her way to the dining hall. Breakfast was self-serve, so she poured some cereal and sat down by herself to eat. She spent that time reliving in her mind every moment she'd spent with Dolly. Maybe she should have caught on at the amusement park, but she'd thought Dolly was just paranoid. Maybe she wasn't. Maybe she had already grown tired of Tommy. But why hadn't she just said so?

No matter how many ways she played it over in her head, there'd been no reason to assume Dolly considered them over until the morning before when she'd told Tommy she didn't respect her and couldn't be in the relationship any longer.

"Fuck her," Tommy muttered. She got up, washed her bowl, and put it in the strainer to dry.

With the whole day ahead of her, she pondered what she could do to help out the greater good of the commune. Certainly stewing in her own self-pity did nothing to help anybody. She decided to go to the vegetable garden and do some weeding. She was the only one there and she found it peaceful and beautiful. Unfortunately, or fortunately, depending on how one looked at it, there were very few weeds to pick. The garden crew had been doing an excellent job.

The sun was rising higher, and it was a beautiful, warm day. People were milling about, getting ready to start their days. Tommy was not alone in her love of sleeping late. Few people were awake before nine.

Tommy walked past Jimmy and a group of people standing around in front of his tent.

"Hey, Jimmy," Tommy said. "Do you know of anything that needs to be done? I'm kind of at a loss of what to do right now."

"I think everything's under control at the moment," Jimmy said.

As a founder of the commune, Tommy didn't have set jobs like so many of the members. She just helped out where she could. And if no one needed help, what on earth was she going to do to keep from thinking about Dolly?

"Well then, what do you say you guys play hooky with me and we go fishing?"

"That sounds great," Jimmy said. He and the others grabbed their fishing gear and met Tommy at her tent. They cut through the tents, out to the forest and to the creek beyond. Tommy felt the warm woodsy air on her and felt alive. She breathed deeply of the scent of the forest. She was home.

The group set about readying their rods for fishing. Tommy was the first one done so she hiked along the edge of the creek a ways before casting. The sight of her line cutting through the water gave her a sense of peace. She loved to fish and normally enjoyed it alone or with a female companion. But she knew she needed company that day so took the four others with her. She knew they'd most likely make too much noise and scare any fish away, but it would still be fun.

Sure enough, people were tangling their lines, losing their hooks and overall being inept at fishing. But it was funny. No one was uptight. Everyone was laughing and enjoying themselves. It was a groovy atmosphere for Tommy. She needed that positive energy.

Tommy and Jimmy each caught two trout and took them back to the dining hall to supplement dinner. Trinity was happy to see them.

"Thank you so much. You know how we all like fresh fish," she said.

"I hope to provide you with a lot more over the next few days."

"Right on. I can't wait."

They'd missed lunch and that was fine. Tommy went back to her tent and took a couple of hits off a joint. She set the joint down just as she heard someone outside her tent.

"Can I come in?" Jimmy said.

"Sure."

"We didn't get to talk out there, but I wanted to check in with you. How you doin'?"

"I'm doin' okay. Not great, but better than yesterday."

"Yeah?" Jimmy said. "I'd guess every day would get a little easier, huh?"

"That's kind of what I'm counting on."

"I'm sure. Well, if you need to talk, the offer still stands."

"I appreciate that."

"Have you thought about showing up at her place of work with a bouquet of flowers and seeing what she does?" Jimmy said.

"It's not that easy."

"Sure it is. What's to stop you? What does she do?"

"She's a nurse."

"Sounds easy enough to me."

Tommy was so tempted to tell Jimmy the truth. He was such a nice guy. She felt that she could trust him. But could she? How would anyone on the commune feel if they found out one of their leaders was consorting with the enemy?

"It does sound easy, but it's not," Tommy finally said.

"Well, maybe I'll come up with an idea that'll be too brilliant for you to turn down."

"Maybe you will." Tommy laughed. "I don't see that happening, but I sure do appreciate your enthusiasm."

Jimmy pulled a joint from his pocket and motioned toward Tommy.

"Sure," Tommy said.

Jimmy took a hit and passed it over. Tommy took a long drag and held it as long as she could. She exhaled slowly as she enjoyed the taste lingering in her mouth.

"That's really good stuff," she said.

"I know. It's killer weed."

Tommy wondered where Jimmy got his. She got hers from a reliable source in the city. And she had more money to spend, so she'd expect hers to be the best. But did she really have more money than Jimmy? No one had any idea how much money she had and she had no idea how much money anybody else had. That was their own business.

"What are you thinking about?" Jimmy said.

"I'm just fucking stoned," Tommy said. "I'm thinking random thoughts. But man, this is good shit."

"You want another hit?"

"I don't think I should."

"I'm going to," Jimmy said. He took another long draw and set the joint in the ashtray.

"Why the fuck not?" Tommy said. She took another hit as well and felt her brain turn to mush.

"So what kind of random thoughts were you thinking?" Jimmy asked.

"Money mostly."

"Money? That's evil. Why would you think about that?"

"Just how no one knows how much anybody has. And how cool that is."

"I like the commune," Jimmy said. "I like everybody working for the common good."

"Me, too."

"Will we be able to live here forever?"

"I plan to," Tommy said. "I don't ever plan to reintegrate into society. They're so fucked up and stupid and hypocritical."

Jimmy laughed.

"Don't hold back. Tell me how you feel."

Tommy started laughing, too.

"Well, it's true. I'd rather be on the outside pointing out their idiocies."

"How can they not see that equal rights for everyone are important?" Jimmy said.

"I can't live in a world like that. I have to be the one leading the revolt, bringing equal rights to the world."

"And then there's the war," Jimmy said.

Tommy grew silent. She thought of Dolly and the ship and the baby killers.

"Hey, man. Don't you agree?" Jimmy said.

"Shit yeah, I agree."

"You sure? You don't seem very adamant."

Tommy dug deep inside. She pulled on every ounce of hate she had for the government for getting them in the war and on every bit of hatred she felt for Dolly for hurting her.

"I'm fucking adamant. Those baby killers. Kids! Just kids from our country going over to that weird world and killing everyone they see. We need to get out of there like yesterday."

"Right on. Now you're talkin'."

"I hate that fucking war, Jimmy. More than you could ever know."

More than anyone could ever know, she thought to herself. She hated the war and Dolly and all they both stood for.

CHAPTER EIGHTEEN

D olly heard the chants as the ship prepared to set sail. She wondered if Tommy was among them, spewing hatred toward all on board. She was sure she had been, even as she hoped she hadn't. She hated the way things ended with her. She wanted them to be able to mail each other letters, to keep in touch and maybe have something after her duty was over. But Tommy never gave her the chance to say that. She had been so angry that Dolly had simply tried to placate her. To no avail.

The first day on the ship there wasn't much going on. They were simply making their way back to Vietnam. They had no wounded yet, but there were a few sick sailors to tend to. Dolly imagined that most of them had bottle flu, but they were in sick bay, so she cared for them nonetheless.

One of the sailors was Carlos Martinez, who Dolly had introduced Tommy to while on liberty. Dolly tried not to have to care for him because she really couldn't stand the man, but one day she had no choice.

"Hey, Samson," he called.

She made her way to his bed with trepidation.

"What can I do for you, Martinez?"

"I've got something I think you need to see." He grabbed his crotch. His shipmates laughed, and Dolly turned bright red from embarrassment and indignation.

"Very funny." She turned to leave.

He slapped her ass. There was more laughter from the crew, and Dolly just fought to keep her stomach from losing its contents. She hated men like Martinez, who only thought of women as sex objects. Didn't he realize she had the same rank as he did and didn't need to put up with his shit?

She went about her business until he called her over again.

"Yes?" she said.

"I think my arm is swollen," he said.

"Really?" He seemed sincere.

"Yeah, my right arm. Will you take a look?"

She had to lean over him to see his arm and almost vomited when she felt his other hand on her breasts. She stood and glared at him.

"What? You got nice tits," he said.

"They're not for you."

"Maybe you should ease up. Life's too short to be so uptight."

She turned to walk away.

"You frigid or something?" he called after her.

She stopped and spun around to face him.

"You have no right to ask me any sort of question like that. It's none of your business."

"It's just that I usually know which nurses put out and I've never heard your name. So I wonder."

She turned her back on him again and went to the rest room where she did throw up. After she had composed herself, she grabbed the supply sheet and began to take inventory. They'd only been at sea for a day, but they'd used supplies, and she wanted to keep on top of them.

There was little to do the first few days at sea, so it was difficult for her to keep her mind off Tommy and the wonderful times they'd had together. She fought tears as she tended to the sick men and often had to disappear to allow herself to regain her composure. Tommy had made her feel alive in a way she never had before. She'd taught her to really enjoy life. And the lovemaking. The lovemaking had been out of this world. She missed it most. As well as the long cuddling after.

Even though she'd been the one to call it off, she really did still love Tommy and knew she always would. At night, in her stateroom, she'd wait until the others were asleep then slide her hand between her legs and think of Tommy and how much she missed her.

She felt like she was simply going through the motions every day at work. She'd tend to sick men and do her daily chores. At night, she'd allow her feelings to wash over her. She was miserable.

One day, she decided to take a few minutes during her down time to write Tommy a letter. Tommy had given Dolly her PO box before they'd split up. Dolly told her again in the letter how much she loved her and how much she wished they could stay in touch. She told her a little about life on the ship, such as it was, and asked her to please write her back. She went to the ship's post office and mailed it. She knew it would be some time before Tommy got it and therefore it would seem like forever before she heard back, assuming she ever would.

The days flowed together, with nothing out of the ordinary happening. The days were filled with daily routine, mostly caring for anybody in sick bay, of which there were very few. Soon they would be back in Vietnam, though, and then there wouldn't be a moment of peace and quiet. In a way, Dolly looked forward to it to get her mind off Tommy.

They arrived off the coast near Da Nang, and Dolly steeled herself for the onslaught of wounded. She was not disappointed. All eight operating rooms were full from the minute they arrived. Dolly worked triage with the other nurses, deciding which patient could wait and which would be seen next. She spent her time trying to stop the bleeding on one patient or another, anything to keep them alive.

After several weeks of triage, Dolly got to work in the aftercare of the patients. It was still brutal, but at least the young men and occasional woman had been treated and were bandaged rather than having their wounds raw and exposed.

On her fourth week there, Dolly was doing her rounds when she came up to a young woman lying in one of the beds. She was sleeping, so Dolly quietly checked her vital signs. As she was doing so, the woman woke up. She opened her eyes, and Dolly felt her breath catch. The woman had the same steel blue eyes as Tommy. She could see that even as the woman's eyes were clouded in pain.

Dolly assumed she would go back to sleep, so went about her business.

"You're like a vision," the woman said.

Dolly stopped adjusting her IV drip and looked at her chart. Her name was Amanda Johnson. She'd had her arm blown off and took shrapnel in her stomach. Her prognosis was good.

"Hi, Amanda," Dolly said.

"And you are?"

Dolly wanted to say Dolly, plain and simple. She wanted to forget protocol and all the navy's rules and regulations and just be Dolly. But she couldn't.

"I'm Lieutenant Samson," she said.

"Nice to meet you."

"Well," Dolly said, "it would have been nice under different circumstances."

"Ain't that the truth?"

"How are you feeling?"

Amanda laughed. It was a laugh devoid of mirth.

"Like I just got out of a war zone."

"Imagine that," Dolly said.

"At least I'll get to go home."

"Well, that's one way to look at it."

"You always got to look for the silver lining."

"I like that. I need to remember that."

"It makes life better," Amanda said.

"I'd imagine it would. It can't be easy, though."

"Not always. Like after your arm gets blown to kingdom come in some jungle in Asia."

Dolly smiled a wry smile at Amanda. She wondered what things would have been like if they'd met in a different situation. One where rank didn't matter. Could they have become friends?

"I need to go check on other patients," Dolly said.

"Oh, of course you do. Thanks for visiting with me."

"I'll be back," Dolly heard herself say.

"That would be great." Amanda closed her eyes, and Dolly made her way around the floor, checking on other wounded kids. Tommy was right. That's all these sailors were. They were boys and girls, too young to be over here suffering like this and dying for no good reason.

Dolly took a deep breath. They were fighting the spread of communism. And that was a reason to be proud of the wounds they had. Somehow, the words rang hollow in her head. Damn Tommy. She had shaken Dolly's beliefs to their core. She hadn't realized it at the time, but Tommy's beliefs had subtly begun to impose themselves on Dolly.

When Dolly got back to Amanda, she was sleeping soundly so Dolly just turned away.

"Lieutenant?"

She turned back.

"I thought you were sleeping," Dolly said.

"That's hard to do here. Did you make your rounds?"

"I did."

"Can you pull up a chair?"

"Sure." Dolly grabbed one and sat next to Amanda.

"So where are you from, Amanda?"

"I'm from Missouri. And you?"

"Georgia."

"What are your dreams for life, Lieutenant?"

Dolly was taken aback. She didn't know how to answer. Was her dream to meet a nice woman and settle down? Or could she be happy with a man?

"Surely you've thought about it," Amanda said. "About what you'll do when this war is over."

"I just always assume I'll be a civilian nurse when this is over."

"Okay, if that what's you want. If that's important to you, then I hope you get to do that."

"And what about you?" Dolly said.

"I've always wanted to be an author. I still think I can. I figure I can type one-handed. I should get pretty good at it over time, don't you think?"

"I suppose you would," Dolly laughed. She liked Amanda's spunk. "What kinds of books would you write?"

"Well, I always thought I would write mystery, but I'm thinking I'd like to write an account of my time here in Nam. Do you think others would want to read that?"

Dolly thought long and hard before answering. On the one hand, people should be interested in what was going on over there. On the other, it might be too much. But she didn't want to discourage Amanda.

"I think there would be an audience," she said.

"Yeah, so do I. Maybe not right now, but in a few years or whenever it's over. Hell, it'll take me that long to type the damned thing."

Dolly came to enjoy her visits with Amanda and was filled with mixed emotions when she heard they were sending her on to a navy hospital in the Philippines. She was stable and would probably be sent stateside from there. She assumed she'd get an honorable discharge at that point. Dolly was happy with her recovery, but was sad to see her go. She stopped by to see her before the helicopter got there.

"Good luck with everything, Amanda."

"Thanks. It's going to feel great to get home."

"Things are different in the states now," Dolly said.

"How so?"

"They're not always welcoming to injured vets."

"They don't have to welcome me," Amanda said. "I'll be home, and that's all that matters to me."

"You just hold on to that." Dolly imagined Tommy and her group greeting poor Amanda and yelling obscenities at her. It filled her with anger. They had no idea who they were yelling at. They didn't know the stories of the kids over here. What right did they have to protest against any of them?

The helicopter arrived and Dolly said good-bye again and went about her business, tending to other injured young men and women. There was usually one injured woman on the ship at any given time. The rest were men. And the injuries were brutal. Dolly much preferred working aftercare to triage, but when it was her time for it, she had no choice.

She hated seeing the kids in pain, having to decide who would be next in the operating room. And it was nearly impossible to explain to them, as they screamed in pain, why they had to wait, why someone else got to go ahead of them. Each person felt their wounds were the worst.

There was so much blood and gore to deal with. She couldn't believe the amount of damage people were able to inflict on one another. How could they do that? Moments like this, she could see things from Tommy's point of view. She wished she could quit thinking about Tommy. She fluctuated from resenting her to agreeing with her and that made her angry. Tommy shouldn't be on her mind while she treated kids fighting for their lives.

Dolly was in her stateroom one afternoon. It was her day off and she was resting on her bunk, replaying the day before and wondering if there was anything more she could have done to save the three men who died as she treated them. It was never easy to lose someone, and three in one day was far from unheard of, but still she played the day over just to be sure.

She heard her name over the P.A. system. She was being called to report to Captain Finley's office. Her stomach was immediately in her throat. What could the C.O. want with her? She made her way through the maze that was the ship's halls and came to his office. She reported in to his assistant and was told to have a seat.

She fidgeted in her chair, nervous and worried about what Captain Finley might need to talk to her about. Was it the deaths the day before? That hardly seemed worthy of a call to the captain's office. Was her overall performance lacking? She didn't think so, but now doubted the job she'd been doing. She felt like she'd been in the waiting area forever before she was finally shown into his office.

Finley stood and motioned to a chair across from his expansive desk. He sat in his leather high-back chair while she tried to get comfortable in a small metal one.

"How are you doing, Samson?" he said.

"Fine, sir."

"Good. I know you've been very busy in the past month or so."

"Yes, sir."

Her stomach got tighter by the moment. Surely he hadn't called her in to just to shoot the breeze. They were both too busy for that. What could he possibly want?

"You know, things are getting dicier on the home front," he said.

"Sir?"

"You know, less support for those of us fighting the good fight against communism."

"Oh, yes, sir."

"There are more and more protests against vets returning home. There are protests and violence directed at recruiting centers. A lot of the people behind these are suspected communists."

Dolly was still confused. She didn't understand what any of this had to do with her.

"I suppose that makes sense, sir."

"Yes, it does. So the navy, well, all the services, have been keeping files on the people behind these acts."

Tommy flashed through Dolly's mind. No, no one could think of her as a communist. She was just another hippie out making sure her voice was heard.

"I'm not sure what any of this has to do with me, sir."

"While you were on liberty, I ran into you in a restaurant. Do you remember that?"

"Yes, sir."

"And who were you with that night? A woman named Tommy, if I'm not mistaken."

"Yes, sir."

"How do you know her?"

Dolly panicked. She certainly couldn't tell the captain she'd picked her up at a bar the first night of liberty. That would mean an immediate discharge for her. And it wouldn't be honorable.

"Samson. I'm waiting. I want to know everything you know about Tommy Benton."

CHAPTER NINETEEN

Tommy settled back in to her life on the commune, eventually almost forgetting the pain Dolly had inflicted. Until the day she went to check on her mail and found a letter from Dolly. The letter professed Dolly's love for her and her wish to remain in contact. Tommy almost crumpled up the paper, but didn't. She read it over and over until the words were imbedded in her brain. She had finally worked herself up to being over Dolly, and this letter just tore the scabs right off the wounds.

She contemplated writing back. She sat at the little table in her tent with pen in hand and tried to come up with exactly what to say. But she didn't know what she wanted to say. She had no idea, as a matter of fact. Ego made her want to tell Dolly to go away and never contact her again. Her heart made her want to tell Dolly she still loved her and would love to keep in touch. Maybe there was a chance, after all, that they would end up together.

But she knew that wasn't the case. Dolly had made it clear that she didn't, couldn't, or wouldn't respect Tommy's life and without that respect they couldn't form a relationship. Not a strong one, anyway. And Dolly had been right. Tommy couldn't respect anyone involved in a war she felt so strongly about.

So Tommy never wrote Dolly back. She finally decided that was the best course of action. Instead, Tommy busied herself and those around her in preparations for Vietnam Moratorium Day. She wanted to get as many people to march on city hall as possible. She also needed to get the word out that, no matter what, it was to be a peaceful, thoughtful demonstration. She contacted a senator who was willing to come speak. He would be a great complement to herself.

She had to organize members of the commune with different chores. Some had to pass out fliers at neighborhood grocery stores. Others had to print up those fliers. Most of them, however were kept busy making signs for everyone to carry. She made sure everyone had something to do to get them ready for October fifteenth.

As the day approached, the energy in the commune was palpable. There was a buzz in the air that was undeniable. Tommy was so excited, her stomach was in knots. Rumor had it that it would be a good turnout. There would be businessmen, lawyers, clergy, and doctors. Or that's what she'd heard anyway. She was thrilled that so many people were willing to speak out against the war.

When the afternoon of the fifteenth arrived, Tommy called the members of the commune together. She climbed on the make shift stage to make a speech.

"Today is a day that we should all be honored to be a part of. All across the nation, people are protesting peacefully against the war we've been so vocally against since the beginning. It's a chance to get our voices heard. It's a chance to become known. And it's a chance to make history.

I want to remind you, instill in you, that this march is to be peaceful. Do not get violent. Anyone who does will be asked to leave the commune. Now, let's march."

The crowd cheered as Tommy led them down the main streets of town, effectively causing traffic snarls as they marched. They moved slowly, with purpose. They kept their heads held high as well as their signs as they made their way toward city hall.

They got to Seaview Square and joined the thousands of others who had come out to peacefully protest. Tommy was so happy she thought she'd explode. There were thousands and thousands of people there. Clearly, the whole town had heard about the protest and were in agreement. She looked around for dissenters, but saw none. She led her group past the rest of them, then led everyone down the street to city hall. The group was so large that it spilled out into the street, which snarled traffic in the heart of the city. There were horns honking and curses yelled, but the group remained calm. Some of them, Tommy noted, even tried to make space for the cars to get through. So much peace filled the air that Tommy truly believed this could end the war. She believed if this kind of peace and solidarity was shown throughout the country, the president would have to pull the troops out.

The senator arrived in his limousine, and the crowd parted to let him and his entourage through. He stood in front of the group and spoke. He thanked everyone for being there and talked about how important it was that we get out of Vietnam. His speech was well written and well practiced, and Tommy was nervous about following him. She had a basic idea of what she was going to say, but it was pretty loose and she hadn't really practiced it. Oh, well, she had no choice. She should have insisted on going first. But the senator had someplace to be so had to go before her, time-wise.

After he finished, the crowd erupted. They shouted and cheered and clapped. The noise was overpowering. Tommy felt small in comparison to this movement she was a part of. The senator welcomed Tommy to the stage, then left the same way he'd come in. Tommy stood in front of all those people and felt slightly overwhelmed. That was unusual for her. She was normally calm and cool at all times during protests. Being in charge was where she was most comfortable. She told herself to calm down. She was Tommy Benton, activist, and this was her chance to make a name for herself on the national level.

She made her off-the-cuff speech and she made it well. She was interrupted several times with cheers so loud she had to stop and get the crowd under control before she continued. She spoke of peace and freedom, of government overstepping. She spoke from her heart, and it was wonderfully received. She stepped off the podium to a rousing round of applause.

Tommy puffed out her chest as she walked back to her friends from the commune. They patted her on her back and shook her hand and hugged her. Everyone told her what a great job she'd done. And she knew they were right. She'd knocked it out of the park. She couldn't wipe the smile off her face. She wanted the rally to go on forever, but knew it was time to call an end to it. People had already started dispersing, so she called to her group and led them back to the commune, where a night of celebrating ensued.

There was music and dancing and drugs. All Tommy's favorite things. While she was swaying to the music, Trinity came over to her and took her hand. They danced together until Trinity pressed against her.

"Take me to bed, Tommy. I need to be with you tonight."

Tommy was high on life and pot, and the idea of a warm body in her bed sounded very good to her. She took Trinity's hand and led her through the crowd. She was suddenly pulled backward and looked around to see Madeline had grabbed hold of Trinity's hand. She stopped.

"Do you know where we're going?" she said to Madeline.

"I'm assuming your tent."

"And you're coming with us?" Tommy said.

"I'd really like to."

"Groovy. Come on."

They made their way through the crowd and came to Tommy's tent. She opened the door for them and admired each of their asses as they passed in front of her. Trinity was slight of build with red hair and freckles. Madeline was medium framed with dark hair and green eyes. Tommy felt her hormones raging at the thought of playing with both of them.

Trinity and Madeline sat on Tommy's bunk while Tommy opened a bottle of Scotch she'd been saving for an occasion such as that day. She couldn't imagine a better time to share it than with these two lovely women.

She found three clean mugs and poured a little into each. She raised hers and toasted.

"To the end of the war."

"Hear, hear," the others said together.

"And to a wonderful night celebrating," Madeline said.

"Mm hm," Trinity said.

They each took a sip. It was fifty-year-old Scotch, and it was smooth as silk going down. Tommy took another sip.

"You should come sit with us," Trinity said.

Tommy sat on the cot next to her. She stroked her hair and felt a twinge she hadn't felt in a long time deep inside her. She wanted these women in the worst way. As she played with Trinity's hair, she felt her pull away and looked to see them kissing. Her loins leapt in excitement. The sight was too much to bear. She pulled Trinity away and kissed her hard on her mouth.

Trinity returned the kiss in kind before turning her head back to Madeline. Tommy watched them kissing and, while excited, felt somehow left out. She knew she could take either one of them at any time, but they seemed to be enjoying each other so much. And then the strangest thing happened. Out of the blue, thoughts of Dolly appeared in her mind. She remembered the nights they'd spent together and the love they had shared. Or Tommy thought they had shared.

Suddenly, the idea of a night with the two women didn't appeal as much. She missed Dolly. There was no way around it. And while she believed in free love, she loved Dolly and until she was over her, she had no desire to be with anyone else.

She moved over to a little chair and watched the women, who seemed oblivious to the fact that she'd moved off the bed. They were lying down, limbs entwined, lost in each other. Tommy let herself out into the night air. The festivities were going strong, but she didn't feel like participating. Then she told herself to snap out of it. This was her night. And while she didn't need to bed the two beauties to celebrate, Dolly couldn't stop her from celebrating in general. She joined the circle and danced and sang with the rest of the commune until the sun came up.

People started slowly making their ways to their tents to get some sleep before starting their days. Tommy didn't want to go back to her tent yet, since she didn't know if the women would still be there. She opted instead, to go to town and pick up a newspaper to see what kind of coverage Vietnam Moratorium Day got.

The paper said that millions of people all over the country had peaceably observed the day. It had been the largest public protest ever on a national scale. There were only a few reported incidents of violence, and those generally were when counter protestors showed up.

Tommy was thrilled with the outcome of the day. She had goose bumps thinking of the small part she played in the big scheme of things. She bought another paper to pass around her commune, but was determined to keep that one for herself.

She made her way back to the commune in a leisurely fashion, still caught up in the enormity of what had happened. When she arrived, people were milling about, reliving the day before and getting ready to start their days. Tommy shared the newspaper with them before heading to her own tent, which thankfully, was empty. She lay down and continued thinking of the day before until she drifted into sleep.

She awoke to a commotion outside her tent. She walked out front to find a newsman and cameraman arguing with Jimmy, who looked at her when she arrived.

"I told them to beat it. I told them to leave you alone."

"It's okay, Jimmy. Thanks, man, but I can handle it now."

"You sure?"

"I'm positive. Thanks again." She turned to the reporter. "How may I help you?"

"You Tommy Benton?" he said.

"I am." All of a sudden, she was nervous. She had been interviewed before. And this reporter seemed nice enough. But the butterflies in her stomach were swarming. She took a deep breath. "How can I help you?"

"We understand you were instrumental in organizing the Vietnam Moratorium Day protest in our town. We'd just like to ask you some questions."

"Sure." Tommy hoped she sounded more confident than she felt. "That would be great."

"Great. Give us a minute to get set up. Did you want to put some makeup on or anything?"

Makeup? Typical male. Women couldn't be attractive without make up. Irritation began to take over where the nerves had been.

"I'm fine. I don't wear makeup."

The reporter looked at her over his shoulder.

"Suit yourself."

When they had things set up to their liking, the camera rolled and the man interviewed her.

"We're here today with Tommy Benton, one of our city's lead activists. Tommy, how does it feel to have been so critical in organizing one of the largest demonstrations in this country's history?" he said.

"It feels fantastic. And the fact that it was mostly peaceful everywhere means a lot to me."

"I suppose I should clarify, you weren't critical in organizing the whole demonstration, just the one here."

"Right. Which still took a lot of work."

"I'm sure it did. You know, Tommy, this isn't the first time we've interviewed you."

"No, it's not."

"I wonder, do you ever plan to take this to a higher level? To maybe make your mark on a national level?"

"I'd love that," she said. "It's definitely one of my goals."

"Do you think this war will last long enough for you to do that?"

"I think this war is pretty much over after yesterday. But we still have a lot of social issues to fight for. So, I do plan to follow my dreams."

"All right, Tommy. Well, thank you for your time. And good luck with your goals."

"Thanks."

The camera was turned off and Tommy breathed a sigh of relief.

"You did great," the cameraman said.

"Thanks."

"You know, I really do believe you'll make it big time someday. I look forward to seeing you on the national news," the reporter said.

"Thanks," Tommy laughed. "I look forward to that, too."

CHAPTER TWENTY

L et's try a different approach," Finley said. "How do you know Benton?"

Dolly continued to ponder her options. She knew she had to say something, and fast.

"We met when we were kids," she lied.

"Really? When?"

"One summer vacation."

"Is that right?" Finley said. "Did your family make a habit of summering in the Hamptons?"

"No, sir."

"I didn't think so. Did you spend vacations in the south of France?"

"No, sir."

"Well then, where exactly did you meet Miss Benton?"

"I don't remember. I just know she's been in my life since I was a kid. When we docked, I decided to look her up."

"You know, she's not just an active communist, she's also a lesbian."

"I didn't know either of those things about her," Dolly said.

"She didn't mention protesting to you?" Finley said.

"She might have mentioned it. Mostly, she took me around and showed me the city."

"So you were seen with a known communist and lesbian publically? That doesn't reflect well on the navy."

"Sir, I'm sure if I didn't know that about her, no one who saw us would have suspected a thing."

"I can't be so sure. Where did you stay in town?"

"I stayed at the Bayside Motel."

"She was seen leaving there in the mornings while you were on liberty. Did she stay with you?"

"No, she lives close by."

"Well, we're clearly not getting anywhere right now, but you need to know that we have reason to believe you were involved with Benton."

"What do you mean, 'involved with'?" Dolly's stomach clenched tightly in a fist. Her bowels felt cold, and she wasn't sure she'd be able to hold them in place.

"We're looking in to all aspects of it, Samson. Whether you went to her commune with her or were romantically involved with her. Either of those will get you discharged. You have to know we take these allegations seriously."

"Wait a minute. What allegations? Who brought any allegations against me? I thought you were investigating Tommy."

"As I said, we have reason to believe you were involved with her. It was brought to our attention. I won't say who, because they have a right to privacy, but they mentioned it to me and it all made sense. You may continue your normal duties at this time, but do know you're under investigation. You're excused."

Dolly stood on shaky legs and walked out of the office. She made her way back to her stateroom and collapsed on her bed, grateful no one else was around. She lay there, shaking, trying to gain her composure. That they were investigating Tommy was one thing, but that she, too, was under investigation was completely unnerving. She'd known that if anyone knew they were together she could get discharged, but try as she might, she couldn't come up with anyone who might have seen them enough to make the connection.

As she lay there, tears traced trails down her cheeks. She was terrified. If she was discharged, where would she go? What would she tell her parents? Would she be able to get a job in a hospital?

All these questions floated through her mind until she fell into a restless sleep. She dreamed of having been discharged and having to wear a special uniform that all dishonorable discharges wore. It made them stand out like pariahs in society. She woke with a start, covered in sweat. She sat up and fought to catch her breath.

"You okay, Dolly?" Tawny was changing out of her nurse's whites and into fatigues.

"Yeah. Bad dream is all."

"Those suck. I'm surprised more of us don't have more of them."

"No kidding. How was the floor today?"

"Busy," Tawny said. "Too busy."

"When is it not?"

"True. It's dinner time. You ready to get some chow?" Tawny said.

Dolly's stomach was still in knots. She thought about refusing.

"You know you'll be hungry later and mess will be closed. Come on," Tawny said.

Dolly got off the bed and straightened her fatigues. She followed Tawny to the mess hall. The place was filled with sailors, and their loud voices threatened to give Dolly a headache. She froze momentarily as she thought of how these people, her brothers and sisters in arms, would turn their backs on her if she were to be discharged dishonorably. She felt nauseous again.

"I think I'm going to pass on dinner," she said.

"Don't be ridiculous. You're here already. Just get in line with me."

Dolly got in line, more so Tawny wouldn't have to eat alone than due to her own hunger. The food smelled worse than usual, and she felt her stomach somersault. She honestly didn't know if she'd be able to hold the food down. She told herself to be strong, that she was merely stressed and didn't even know if Finley would be able to find enough evidence against her. She needed to just relax and live her days as she had all the ones previously.

They got to the food and Dolly took a little, prompting Tawny to comment.

"That's hardly enough for a bird. You need more." She scooped more food on Dolly's plate and they found open spots at a table.

"So what's really going on with you?" Tawny said. "It's more than just a bad dream."

"I can't say," Dolly said.

"Come on. Look at all we've been through together. Certainly you can talk to me about what's bugging you."

"It's kind of personal."

"Again, look at what we've been through. I know your most intimate secrets."

"And now, Finley's trying to discover them," Dolly said.

"Huh? What do you mean?"

"I met with him today. He's investigating me, Tawny."

"Oh, shit. That's not good. What prompted that?"

"Tommy and I ran into him at a restaurant. Apparently, he recognized her or something. I don't know. All I know is they have a file on her. They say she's a known communist and a lesbian."

"But you're not a communist. You're serving on this ship. You help hundreds every week. What communist would do that?"

"No, I don't think that's their concern. He said someone alleged that Tommy and I were involved."

"Oh, shit," Tawny said again. "That's really bad. That's a strong allegation. Who would have said anything?"

"That's just it. I can't figure out who would have reason to say anything. I've thought and thought and can't come up with anyone."

"Well, if you do, let me know. Maybe we can talk to them, get them to recant."

"That would be wonderful, Tawny, but I doubt they would. If they've made allegations, they've clearly got something against me to begin with. What I was doing with Tommy didn't hurt anybody."

"No, it didn't. It was between you and her. Nobody else was even involved. Who the fuck would have said anything?"

"I don't know. The only one who knew for sure was you, and you wouldn't have said anything," Dolly said.

"No. Even if I didn't love you like a sister, it would be a bit like the pot calling the kettle black."

"Exactly. I don't know. I guess it really doesn't matter who said something. I just need to hope Finley gives up on me and focuses his attention on something else."

"I hope so, too. But I still want to know who could have said something. Who did you see on liberty?"

"Finley. I think that's all."

"What did you do every day? Think back to that and who might have seen you."

"Oh shit, Martinez," Dolly said.

"What?"

"We saw Martinez at the amusement park and then at dinner that night."

"Well, that doesn't mean you're gay, but Martinez is an asshole, so might have said something."

"Yeah, but there's more." Dolly felt stupid even as she said it.

"What?"

"He saw us going into the Tunnel of Love together." She felt the pit in her stomach grow. How could she have been so foolish as to agree to go on that ride with Tommy?

"Oh, that's not good," Tawny said. "That's kind of incriminating."

"I told Tommy I didn't want to go on it," Dolly said. "But she was insisting I was being paranoid. So I gave in and went on the ride. We saw Martinez getting off just as we got on."

"Shit," Tawny said. "I don't know what to say except shit."

"And he's such an asshole. Do you know that when we first started back over here, he asked if I was frigid?"

"Why? And what business is it of his?"

"He said he's never heard stories of me messing around. Which of course he hasn't."

"What a dick."

"I know. Oh, Tawny. What will I do if he ruins my life?"

"It won't be the end of your life, for starters. You'll just end up in a civilian hospital somewhere. Wherever you choose. You won't be dealing with kids being blown to smithereens every day. It's not a bad thing."

Dolly was just about to respond when Martinez and his friends walked by.

"Whatcha munchin' on, Samson? They servin' carpet tonight?"

Dolly sat silently fuming. She didn't move or even speak until she heard them walk off.

"Oh my God," Tawny said. "I can't believe he said that to you."

"I'm telling you. He's so fucking inappropriate with me. But what can I do?"

"True. There's nothing to do. Which is wrong."

"Tell me about it," Dolly said.

"So, what are you going to do?" Tawny said. "About the allegations and everything?"

"What can I do? Hope Finley sides with me, and in the meantime, just keep doing my job."

"Well, I'm always here for you if you need to talk."

"Thanks."

They went back to their stateroom and Dolly climbed onto her bunk again.

"Don't you want to go see what kind of games are being played?" Tawny said. When dinner was done, the mess hall turned into a gathering place, with people playing various games or just hanging out.

"Not tonight. I'm gonna crawl into bed and pull the covers over my head and forget I'm alive."

"Not sure how healthy that is, but I'm not sure I blame you, either."

"Thanks." Dolly climbed off the bed and undressed. She put on her pajamas and climbed back in.

"You want me to say something to Martinez?"

"No, thanks," Dolly said. "Let's just hope he burns in some eternal hell."

Tawny left and Dolly lay under her covers wishing she had some recourse to all that was happening to her. She didn't, though. Homosexuality was grounds for immediate dismissal. And if Finley felt there was enough evidence, then dismissal was coming and there was nothing she could do about it.

She heard Tawny come back and wondered what time it was, but kept to herself because she didn't want to talk about it anymore. She wondered how long she'd been lying awake and thought how lousy she'd feel in the morning if she didn't get some sleep.

It was Dolly's last day on triage. She was ordering the gurneys for surgery based on injuries. One young man was covered in shrapnel on his arms and legs and stomach. She knew he wasn't critical, so moved him toward the end of the line.

"Why are you putting me here? I need help," he said.

"We're going to get you that help," she said. "What's your name, son?"

"Marcus. Marcus Bremer."

"Okay, Marcus. I know you feel like you're a long way from the operating room, but they're quick in there."

"But I fucking hurt."

"I know you do. Hold on and I'll get you something for the pain."

She went to the nurse's station and got a syringe of morphine. She took it back to him.

"Oh, shit," he said. "I hate needles."

"You won't even notice it," Dolly said.

"Bullshit."

"Tell me about yourself, Marcus. How old are you?"

"I'm nineteen." He never took his eyes off the needle in her hand.

"And where are you from?"

"Saginaw."

"Oh wow. It gets cold there, doesn't it?"

"Yeah. It's nothing like here."

"What do you miss most about home?"

He leaned his head back as he thought, and Dolly jammed the needle in his arm.

"Ouch," he said.

"Oh, come on, it wasn't that bad."

"Not compared to everything else I've got going on."

"You just relax now, Marcus, and we'll get you into surgery as soon as we can."

She worked all day with casualties, losing some, but keeping most alive at least long enough to get into the operating room. She was exhausted when her day finally ended. She and Tawny went to the mess hall, and then Dolly fell sound asleep, too tired to even worry about things.

The next day, she was doing her rounds when she came upon Marcus.

"Good morning. How are you feeling today?"

"Like I got blown to hell."

Dolly nodded.

"That makes sense. But at least you have all your parts, right?"

"No, shit. Although I'm guessing that also means I get to go back out and fight some more in a few days, huh?"

"I honestly don't know how that works," she said. "But I would imagine if you did get sent back out it would be after more than a few days."

"I don't want to go back out there," Marcus said.

"I don't blame you."

"It's fucking scary."

"I'm sure it is," she said. "It's scary enough on this ship seeing what's been done to you guys. I can't imagine actually being on the front line."

"It sucks."

Dolly wanted to hear more. She wanted to agree with him, to tell him that she hated seeing all the young men come in here all blown to pieces, but she didn't. She couldn't. If anyone overheard, it could make her sound anti-war, which would be dubbed pro-communist if it got back to Finley.

"I need to go check on other patients," she told him. "I'll be back to chat more later."

"That would be great."

She made her rounds and found everyone as expected. Most were in some level of pain and several were running fevers. She found the doctor and had him come check them. Some went back to surgery. One died. It was a long day. She went back to talk to Marcus.

"How you doin?" she said.

"Okay. I hurt, but I guess that's just part of the deal."

Dolly knew there was no way to take away the full amount of pain, but she did her best to keep her patients comfortable.

"Do you need something for it?"

"No. It's not that bad. Just kind of annoying right now. Maybe later I will."

She checked his chart. Yes, he'd be due in another hour.

"You'll get more in an hour, so just be strong."

"I kind of wish I'd been hurt worse, so I'd get discharged," Marcus said.

"Yes, but you don't wish you'd have to go through life with one arm or one leg."

"No, I don't. But I really don't want to go back out there. Can you do anything? Say anything to make it so I don't go back?"

"I'm sorry, Marcus. That would be up to the doctors. I have no say in it. I'm really sorry."

"That's life," he said.

The next day when Dolly was making her rounds, she found Marcus's bed occupied by another young man. She was confused. Marcus was nowhere near ready to be transported off the ship. She pulled his chart. Suicide.

"Damn it!"

"What's up?" Tawny said.

"We just lost another one to suicide. A nice, likeable young guy."

"It's hell out there, Dolly. Kids'll do anything not to have to go back."

"I get that. Still…" She had nothing more to say. The weight of the war caused her shoulders to sag. She wondered what the hell they were doing out there. Why did these kids have to die? She shook her head. She sounded like Tommy. She reminded herself why they were there and why she was there. She was patriotic and believed in her government. Or did she?

After her shift, she went back to her stateroom and changed into fatigues. She went up to the deck to get some fresh air. That's when she heard the page. It was calling her back to Finley's office.

She braced herself, unsure of what was coming, but terrified it would be the worst. She pictured a court-martial in her future and didn't know if she'd be able to stand the trial. She wanted to jump off the ship and swim to shore to escape whatever Finley had to say. But that wasn't rational and Dolly knew it. She walked down below to the captain's office.

Once again, she was made to sit in the small waiting area. She assumed that was to give her time to gather her thoughts, but that was impossible. Her thoughts were all over the board. She didn't want a dishonorable discharge and didn't think she deserved one. But it wasn't up to her. It was up to Captain Finley.

She was finally called into his office, and once again he motioned her to sit in the uncomfortable metal chair across from his expansive desk.

"We've concluded our investigation, Samson," he said with no preamble.

"Yes, sir?"

"And we believe you were involved in a homosexual relationship with Tommy Benton."

"But—"

"No buts, Samson. We've reached our conclusion. As you know, the navy believes homosexuality to be a mental disease. We cannot tolerate it in our ranks. Now, we're not going to court-martial you so you won't get a dishonorable discharge, but you will get an undesirable discharge. Do you understand?"

Dolly sat fighting tears. She was getting kicked out. There was nothing she could do.

"Yes, sir."

"There's a helicopter waiting on deck. It'll take you to the airbase at Da Nang. From there you go back to the states. Go pack your stateroom. I don't want a speck of anything of yours left behind. Get going. The bird leaves in fifteen minutes."

"Yes, sir."

Dolly went back to her room, tears streaming down her face. She didn't try to hide it. Her world was crashing in around her. She had nowhere to go and no one to talk to. She couldn't tell her parents. She couldn't tell her friends. She was lost. She packed her duffle bag, made sure her area looked unoccupied and headed to the deck and the waiting transport.

CHAPTER TWENTY-ONE

Tommy had just returned from fishing in the creek. She had only caught a few fish, but the time on the creek was always so peaceful. She took the fish to the dining hall and wandered back to her tent. It was a beautiful day. The sky was bright blue and the temperature was in the mid seventies. She loved days like that. She was happy. Life was good.

She lay down on her bunk and closed her eyes to take a nap.

"Excuse me. Tommy, are you home?"

She sat up in bed. That voice. No way. She went to the door of her tent and opened it. There stood Dolly, a duffle bag on her back and eyes swollen. Her heart went out to her briefly before she remembered the pain Dolly had inflicted on her. She was cool.

"What are you doing here?"

"I'm sorry to bother you, but I don't have any place else to go."

"Are you on liberty again so soon?"

"No, Tommy. I got kicked out."

"You *what*?"

"I got an undesirable discharge," Dolly said.

"What does that mean?"

"It's not as bad as a dishonorable discharge, but it's close. I still won't get any of my rights or privileges."

"So you were court-martialed or something?"

"No. That requires a trial, and I think Finley didn't want to deal with that."

"Well, couldn't you have demanded one?" Tommy said.

"And have people dredge up my personal life? No, thanks. The result would have been the same. Only I could have ended up with a dishonorable discharge. Mine's not that bad."

"I still don't understand," Tommy said. "What were you kicked out for?"

"Being a lesbian."

"What?"

"They have a file on you, Tommy. You're a known communist and a known lesbian."

"I'm not a communist." Tommy was adamant about that, though secretly happy to know the military had a file on her. She must be doing something right.

"Well," Dolly said, "in their minds you are."

Tommy felt guilty. Her heart fell when she realized what Dolly was saying.

"So you got kicked out because of me?"

"Because of my involvement with you as a lesbian. Yes."

Tommy sat on her bed.

"I'm so sorry, Dolly. I never wanted that to happen."

"I was worried it would. And it did. Still, I wouldn't have given up that time with you."

Tommy was confused. Had it all been real to Dolly after all? If not, why would she have come here to find her? Had she really called it off because she was scared of just this happening?

"So now what are you going to do?" Tommy said.

"I have no idea. I was hoping I could crash with you for a while while I figure things out."

Tommy was torn. She wanted to say yes, but still didn't know if she trusted her.

"I'm even willing to go on protests against the war," Dolly said. "I've seen so much, Tommy. You can't imagine the damage done to our young men and women over there."

"I can imagine. That's why I'm against it. We have no right to be over there and those kids are paying a price for nothing."

"I agree," Dolly said softly.

"You do?"

"I do."

"Wow. Okay. I never expected to hear you say that."

"I never thought I'd be in a position to," Dolly said.

"Let's go for a walk. Set your stuff down anywhere."

"Does that mean I can stay?"

"I'm still not sure. You hurt me in a way no one else ever has, Dolly. You need to understand that."

"And you need to understand I had to do it so this wouldn't happen," Dolly said.

"And yet it did."

"Yes. It did."

Dolly set her duffle bag on the floor across the tent from Tommy's cot. She followed Tommy out of the tent and through the maze of tents until they came to a clearing. Tommy led her to the banks of the creek and sat on a rock. Dolly did the same.

"I'm confused, Dolly. You're the last person I thought would show up at my tent. Today or any day. I didn't write you back on purpose, Dolly. The way you left made me want you out of my life forever."

"If you had listened to me, you'd have known that wasn't what I wanted."

"No. You wanted it both ways. And that was even worse," Tommy said. "But now you're back. And you got kicked out of doing what you love because of me. I feel guilty. But if I let you stay with me, I don't want it to be out of guilt."

"Neither do I," Dolly said. "I want it to be out of feelings for me. At least feelings of friendship, if not more."

"Do you understand that you're the only woman I've ever loved?" Tommy said. "Do you really grasp that?"

"And you're the only woman I've ever loved."

"Well, you had a funny way of showing it when you left."

"What if I hadn't called it off, Tommy? What then? Would you have walked me to the ship to say good-bye? Hell no. You'd still be standing with your group yelling hateful things, knowing full well I was on that ship. That was the whole thing. We were on two different sides of a major issue. That didn't mean I didn't love you."

"So now we're on the same page so I should take you back and we can live happily ever after?"

"Tommy, I get it that you're still angry with me," Dolly said. "And I won't ask for forever. I can't really, can I? But I really do need a place to stay while I figure out what to do with my life and you are the first person I thought of."

"I can't imagine why you thought of me. After the way you left things."

"I guess I wanted a chance to prove to you that I do love you."

"Do or did?" Tommy said.

"Both, I suppose."

"Both?"

"Yes, Tommy. I never quit loving you. I looked for a letter from you every day on that ship. I never gave up hope. I still love you, but I'll understand if you don't love me. If you can just accept me as a friend, I'll be happy."

"I'm still so blown away. I heard your voice at my tent and I thought 'it can't be.' And even as I thought that, I wanted it to be," Tommy said.

"Tommy, think of all the good times we had while I was on liberty. We had a groovy time together. You have to admit that."

"It was groovy, yes, but it wasn't real life. It was a lifetime of love compacted into three days. We made love all the time and played tourist. It wasn't real life. Real life to me is living in a tent and protesting social injustices. What's real life for you, Dolly?"

"I don't know. Can't you understand that? That's what I need to figure out. My real life was supposed to be planned out for me in the navy. I didn't have to question it. Real life meant helping injured and dying kids on a ship. That was ripped from me. I have no idea what my life looks like now," Dolly said.

"What do you think it does?"

"I'm hoping to get a job as a nurse somewhere. But I don't know that anyone would hire me with an undesirable discharge."

"Yeah, I'm sure that would be tough."

"But I meant what I said. I'd be willing to go on protest marches with you, Tommy."

"You can't be a nurse and live on a commune. I don't think that would work."

"No. I don't think so, either. But as I said, I don't know that I could find a job as a nurse right now anyway."

"So, this is just a temporary stop for you? I'm a temporary stop?" Tommy said.

"I don't want you to be a temporary stop. Couldn't we have a smaller commune in an old house somewhere?"

"Maybe. Someday. Not now, though."

"No, not now," Dolly said.

Tommy stood and extended her hand to help Dolly up.

"So, can I stay?" Dolly said.

"Yes, you can stay. For as long as you like. And I forgive you for the way you left things when you had to report back to duty. I understand now the consequences you were facing. I'm sorry I doubted the severity of them."

Dolly moved closer to Tommy, and Tommy found it hard to breathe with her so close. She felt her arms go around Dolly of their own accord. She pulled her close and lowered her lips to taste hers. Her head spun as their lips met. Her hesitancy melted away, followed by a need she had denied for too long.

Tommy slipped her tongue along Dolly's lower lip, and Dolly opened her mouth to welcome it. Dolly was warm and moist, and Tommy couldn't wait to find the rest of her that way.

"Let's get back to my tent," Tommy said.

"Yes. Let's."

Tommy held her hand the whole way back to her tent. When they arrived, she closed her tent door securely.

"Are you going to be able to do this here?" Tommy said.

"I have to. I couldn't stop right now even if I wanted to."

"Good."

Tommy eased Dolly back on her cot and climbed on top of her. She wanted to ravish her, but forced herself to go slowly. It had been so long, she wanted to savor every moment. Tommy unbuttoned one button, then another on Dolly's blouse. She kissed every inch of exposed skin with each new button opened.

Dolly's skin was soft and warm and she smelled like sunshine and fresh air. Tommy continued to go at an easy pace as she peeled Dolly's shirt off and lay looking at her beautiful breasts held snugly in her bra. She kissed and sucked on the exposed flesh before reaching around to unhook her bra, setting the full breasts free.

Tommy suckled first one and then the other nipple, listening to Dolly's sharp intake of breath each time. She loved Dolly's breasts and had missed them terribly. She skimmed her hand along the length of Dolly's body, watching the goose flesh erupt as she did. Her body was so responsive and felt so nice under Tommy's touch. She continued to touch every inch of her until she could take it no longer.

She unbuttoned Dolly's slacks and unzipped them, then pulled them off. Only Dolly's panties stood in the way of pure pleasure. She pressed the crotch of the panties against Dolly and felt how wet and warm she was. She was as ready for Tommy as Tommy was for her. She stripped them away and moved her hand to her clit.

It was slick, so very slick and she knew she had to taste her. She climbed between her legs and licked the hardened nerve center until Dolly cried out. But Tommy wasn't done yet. She licked her all over before going back to her clit. She slid her fingers inside and stroked at the silky area she found there. In no time, Dolly was crying out again.

Still, Tommy didn't quit. She continued over and over until Dolly had to tap her shoulder.

"No more. I can't take any more," she said weakly.

Tommy moved up on the cot and took Dolly into her arms. She fell asleep with the knowledge that she'd never let her go again.

About the Author

MJ Williamz was raised on California's central coast, which she left at age seventeen to pursue an education. She graduated from Chico State, and it was in Chico that she rediscovered her love of writing. It wasn't until she moved to Portland, however, that her writing really took off, with the publication of her first short story in 2003. She hasn't looked back.

MJ is the author of nine books, including the award-winning *Initiation by Desire* and *Escapades*. She has also had over thirty short stories published, most of them erotica, with a few romances and a few horrors thrown in for good measure.

MJ now lives in Houston with her wife and son.

Visit MJ's website at www.mjwilliamz.com to keep up with her or friend her on Facebook.

Books Available from Bold Strokes Books

Camp Rewind by Meghan O'Brien. A summer camp for grown-ups becomes the site of an unlikely romance between a shy, introverted divorcee and one of the Internet's most infamous cultural critics—who attends undercover. (978-1-62639-793-4)

Cross Purposes by Gina L. Dartt. In pursuit of a lost Acadian treasure, three women must not only work out the clues, but also the complicated tangle of emotion and attraction developing between them. (978-1-62639-713-2)

Imperfect Truth by C.A. Popovich. Can an imperfect truth stand in the way of love? (978-1-62639-787-3)

Life in Death by M. Ullrich. Sometimes the devastating end is your only chance for a new beginning. (978-1-62639-773-6)

Love on Liberty by MJ Williamz. Hearts collide when politics clash. (978-1-62639-639-5)

Serious Potential by Maggie Cummings. Pro golfer Tracy Allen plans to forget her ex during a visit to Bay West, a lesbian condo community in NYC, but when she meets Dr. Jennifer Betsy, she gets more than she bargained for. (978-1-62639-633-3)

Taste by Kris Bryant. Accomplished chef Taryn has walked away from her promising career in the city's top restaurant to devote her life to her five-year-old daughter and is content until Ki Blake comes along. (978-1-62639-718-7)

The Second Wave by Jean Copeland. Can star-crossed lovers have a second chance after decades apart, or does the love of a lifetime only happen once? (978-1-62639-830-6)

Valley of Fire by Missouri Vaun. Taken captive in a desert outpost after their small aircraft is hijacked, Ava and her captivating passenger discover things about each other and themselves that will change them both forever. (978-1-62639-496-4)

Basic Training of the Heart by Jaycie Morrison. In 1944, socialite Elizabeth Carlton joins the Women's Army Corps to escape family expectations and love's disappointments. Can Sergeant Gale Rains get her through Basic Training with their hearts intact? (978-1-62639-818-4)

Before by KE Payne. When Tally falls in love with her band's new recruit, she has a tough decision to make. What does she want more—Alex or the band? (978-1-62639-677-7)

Believing in Blue by Maggie Morton. Growing up gay in a small town has been hard, but it can't compare to the next challenge Wren—with her new, sky-blue wings—faces: saving two entire worlds. (978-1-62639-691-3)

Coils by Barbara Ann Wright. A modern young woman follows her aunt into the Greek Underworld and makes a pact with Medusa to win her freedom by killing a hero of legend. (978-1-62639-598-5)

Courting the Countess by Jenny Frame. When relationship-phobic Lady Henrietta Knight starts to care about housekeeper Annie Brannigan and her daughter, can she overcome her fears and promise Annie the forever that she demands? (978-1-62639-785-9)

Dapper by Jenny Frame. Amelia Honey meets the mysterious Byron De Brek and is faced with her darkest fantasies, but will her strict moral upbringing stop her from exploring what she truly wants? (978-1-62639-898-6E)

Delayed Gratification: The Honeymoon by Meghan O'Brien. A dream European honeymoon turns into a winter storm nightmare involving a delayed flight, a ditched rental car, and eventually, a surprisingly happy ending. (978-1-62639-766-8E)

For Money or Love by Heather Blackmore. Jessica Spaulding must choose between ignoring the truth to keep everything she has, and doing the right thing only to lose it all—including the woman she loves. (978-1-62639-756-9)

Hooked by Jaime Maddox. With the help of sexy Detective Mac Calabrese, Dr. Jessica Benson is working hard to overcome her past, but it may not be enough to stop a murderer. (978-1-62639-689-0)

Lands End by Jackie D. Public relations superstar Amy Kline is dealing with a media nightmare, and the last thing she expects is for restaurateur Lena Michaels to change everything, but she will. (978-1-62639-739-2)

Lysistrata Cove by Dena Hankins. Jack and Eve navigate the maelstrom of their darkest desires and find love by transgressing gender, dominance, submission, and the law on the crystal blue Caribbean Sea. (978-1-62639-821-4)

Twisted Screams by Sheri Lewis Wohl. Reluctant psychic Lorna Dutton doesn't want to forgive, but if she doesn't do just that an innocent woman will die. (978-1-62639-647-0)

A Class Act by Tammy Hayes. Buttoned-up college professor Dr. Margaret Parks doesn't know what she's getting herself into when she agrees to one date with her student, Rory Morgan, who is 15 years her junior. (978-1-62639-701-9)

Bitter Root by Laydin Michaels. Small town chef Adi Bergeron is hiding something, and Griffith McNaulty is going to find out what it is even if it gets her killed. (978-1-62639-656-2)

Capturing Forever by Erin Dutton. When family pulls Jacqueline and Casey back together, will the lessons learned in eight years apart be enough to mend the mistakes of the past? (978-1-62639-631-9)

Deception by VK Powell. DEA Agent Colby Vincent and Attorney Adena Weber are embroiled in a drug investigation involving homeless veterans and an attraction that could destroy them both. (978-1-62639-596-1)

Dyre: A Knight of Spirit and Shadows by Rachel E. Bailey. With the abduction of her queen, werewolf-bodyguard Des must follow the kidnappers' trail to Europe, where her queen—and a battle unlike any Des has ever waged—awaits her. (978-1-62639-664-7)

First Position by Melissa Brayden. Love and rivalry take center stage for Anastasia Mikhelson and Natalie Frederico in one of the most prestigious ballet companies in the nation. (978-1-62639-602-9)

Best Laid Plans by Jan Gayle. Nicky and Lauren are meant for each other, but Nicky's haunting past and Lauren's societal fears threaten to derail all possibilities of a relationship. (987-1-62639-658-6)

Exchange by CF Frizzell. When Shay Maguire rode into rural Montana, she never expected to meet the woman of her dreams—or to learn Mel Baker was held hostage by legal agreement to her right-wing father. (987-1-62639-679-1)

Just Enough Light by AJ Quinn. Will a serial killer's return to Colorado destroy Kellen Ryan and Dana Kingston's chance at love, or can the search-and-rescue team save themselves? (987-1-62639-685-2)

Rise of the Rain Queen by Fiona Zedde. Nyandoro is nobody's princess. She fights, curses, fornicates, and gets into as much trouble as her brothers. But the path to a throne is not always the one we expect. (987-1-62639-592-3)

Tales from Sea Glass Inn by Karis Walsh. Over the course of a year at Cannon Beach, tourists and locals alike find solace and passion at the Sea Glass Inn. (987-1-62639-643-2)

The Color of Love by Radclyffe. Black sheep Derian Winfield needs to convince literary agent Emily May to marry her to save the Winfield Agency and solve Emily's green card problem, but Derian didn't count on falling in love. (987-1-62639-716-3)

A Reluctant Enterprise by Gun Brooke. When two women grow up learning nothing but distrust, unworthiness, and abandonment, it's no wonder they are apprehensive and fearful when an overwhelming love just won't be denied. (978-1-62639-500-8)

Above the Law by Carsen Taite. Love is the last thing on Agent Dale Nelson's mind, but reporter Lindsey Ryan's investigation could change the way she sees everything—her career, her past, and her future. (978-1-62639-558-9)

Jane's World: The Case of the Mail Order Bride by Paige Braddock. Jane's PayBuddy account gets hacked and she inadvertently purchases a mail order bride from the Eastern Bloc. (978-1-62639-494-0)

Love's Redemption by Donna K. Ford. For ex-convict Rhea Daniels and ex-priest Morgan Scott, redemption lies in the thin line between right and wrong. (978-1-62639-673-9)

The Shewstone by Jane Fletcher. The prophetic Shewstone is in Eawynn's care, but unfortunately for her, Matt is coming to steal it. (978-1-62639-554-1)